KISS AND TELL

"You're not even listening to me."

Denise raised her eyebrows. "I'm sorry, Britt. But the more I think about Pete—"

"The sadder you get?"

"Mmm—and something else, too." Denise sat up straighter. "You know what? I think Pete's acting like a real jerk. We've been going out for three months and he doesn't even trust me enough to listen to my explanation! He just dumps me." She snapped her fingers. "Like that!"

"That's pretty rotten," Britt agreed. "If my boy-friend ever did that to me—"

"What would you do?" Denise asked curiously.

"I'd cry," Britt replied honestly. "But then I'd get pretty mad."

Denise nodded. She felt that spark of anger in her grow. Who did Pete think he was, anyway?

Bantam Sweet Dreams Romances
Ask your bookseller for the books you have missed

Kiss and Tell

Shannon Blair

BANTAM BOOKS

TORONTO · NEW YORK · LONDON · SYDNEY · AUCKLAND

RL 5, IL age 11 and up

KISS AND TELL
A Bantam Book / August 1985

*Sweet Dreams and its associated logo are registered trademarks of
Bantam Books, Inc. Registered in U.S. Patent and Trademark Office
and elsewhere.*

Cover photo by Pat Hill

*Bantam Books are published by Bantam Books, Inc. Its trademark,
consisting of the words "Bantam Books" and the portrayal of
a rooster, is Registered in U.S. Patent and Trademark Office
and in other countries. Marca Registrada. Bantam Books, Inc.,
666 Fifth Avenue, New York, New York 10103.*

PRINTED IN THE UNITED STATES OF AMERICA

O   0 9 8 7 6 5 4 3 2 1

For Ben, with appreciation

Chapter One

The locker room was in a state of chaos as girls jostled for spaces in front of the mirror that ran along one wall.

"Excuse me," Denise Taylor murmured as she edged her way closer to the mirror. "Uh, excuse me, please."

No one replied or moved. Finally one girl stepped aside slightly to give Denise a little room.

"Thanks," Denise said. She might as well have saved her voice, she thought. The girl didn't even acknowledge her presence.

At least her own reflection in the mirror assured Denise that she wasn't totally invisible—though she might as well have been as far as this group was concerned. It had been three months since she had transferred to Lakeside High, but she doubted that even one girl among the thirty or more in the room knew her name.

She looked down the mirror at the row of girls fumbling with lipsticks and hairbrushes, chattering and laughing, and she thought about how much she envied them. She pulled her own hairbrush out of her purse and silently pulled it through her short blond hair.

She gazed at her reflection sternly. *It's your own fault*, she told herself. *So don't feel sorry for yourself. You haven't made any effort to get to know these kids, so don't complain if none of them talks to you.* She tried to focus on the little brush in her hand but could only see her sad, deep-set blue eyes as she overheard the conversation that was going on behind her.

"I can't believe you broke up with him, Ingrid. Britt's party is next week, and the prom's only six weeks away. What are you going to do for a date?"

Denise couldn't see the speaker, but she had a clear view in the mirror of the other girl, Ingrid. She was tall, with hair that looked too red to be real, and she had on a lot of green eye shadow. She shrugged and made a "who cares" face.

"I was getting bored with Billy," she

drawled. "I'm sick of these Mister-Nice-Guy types, you know? I'll find somebody else."

"It's not that easy, Ingrid," the other voice warned. "You don't find cute guys like Billy behind every tree. If you're not careful, you're going to end up without anybody to go with."

Denise tossed her brush back in her bag and pulled out her pink blusher. *Well, at least I don't have* that *to worry about,* she thought contentedly as she lightly swept the brush across her cheekbones. I'll *always have someone to go out with. As long as Pete's around, anyway.*

And, as always, the mere thought of Pete lifted her spirits and made her forget her loneliness. Pete! How lucky she was to have a boy like that in her life. The faces in the mirror blurred as she mentally pictured the love of her life. He was tall, but not too tall; slender, but not skinny. His eyes were brown with flecks of gold in them, and his wavy, light brown hair was so soft that Denise constantly felt tempted to run her fingers through it. But there was more to Pete than just his good looks. He had warmth and a marvelously dry sense of humor. And she knew she could trust him. Unlike other girls who always worried whether or not their boyfriends liked them, Denise *knew* that Pete loved her.

"Hey, how about moving over?"

Ingrid was glaring at her. She gripped a black eyeliner as if it were a weapon. Denise hastily gathered up her makeup bag and purse.

"Excuse me," she muttered, for what must have been the zillionth time in three months, and edged back, away from the mirror and out of the crowd.

The halls were bustling as she slowly made her way to sociology class. As usual, the noisy hallways made her feel anonymous. And, as usual, she masked those feelings by thinking about Pete. If not for Pete, she'd be totally alone.

She'd met him on her very first day at Lakeside High. Tired of city living, her parents had moved the family from Chicago to the suburbs right after Christmas. Denise had protested strongly, but to no avail. In the big, crowded city she had felt so comfortable. But then, she'd been born there, and her high-school friends were kids she'd known since childhood. Now, here she was in a cozy, casual little village, and it might as well have been a foreign country as far as Denise was concerned. She just didn't belong.

Her thoughts drifted back to that first day of school, and she relived it. . . .

* * *

How ill at ease she felt! Everyone seemed to know everyone else, and she knew no one. She stood at her new locker for at least fifteen minutes, almost bursting into tears as the combination of her lock refused to work. A harsh voice came from behind her.

"Hey, what are you doing at my locker?"

She whirled around to face a boy who would have been very good-looking if he hadn't looked so annoyed.

"It's—it's *my* locker," she managed to say. "But the combination won't work."

His eyes searched her face, and his expression softened. "Are you new here?"

Silently, she nodded.

"Well," he said, and his voice was gentler, "this is definitely my locker. The office gave you the wrong one. You'd better go back there and check it out."

Wordlessly, she nodded again. And then he smiled.

"I'll go with you."

He'd been going with her ever since. Pete had transferred to Lakeside only six months before she had, and he didn't know many people either. But he didn't seem to care. He was a loner by nature—not unfriendly, but the kind of guy who just didn't like to hang around with a group. He wasn't into sports or school activities. He liked to read, fool around with his home computer, and be with Denise.

And that was fine with Denise. As long as she had Pete, she felt she didn't have to knock herself out trying to make friends.

But as she walked into the classroom and saw all the other kids casually perched on desks, talking to one another, she thought wistfully of the friends she had left behind in the city. Lately she'd been wishing she had at least one girlfriend here. Pete was wonderful, but sometimes a girl needed another girl to talk to, to share secrets with, someone lively and fun—like that girl who sat next to her in class, Britt Leland.

She was one of the few kids who ever went out of her way to speak to Denise. Not that Denise really knew her, though. Britt was one of the most popular girls at Lakeside, always surrounded by a crowd of friends.

Usually Britt had a friendly "hi" for Denise when she came into class, but that day she seemed oblivious to Denise. She was bent over the sociology textbook, madly trying to cram before the quiz they would be having in a few minutes. Her absolutely straight, long brown hair, cut fashionably blunt, fell over her face, partially hiding her clear brown eyes and cute, turned-up nose.

The bell rang just then, and Britt looked up. She caught Denise's eye and grinned ruefully.

"I am definitely not prepared for this test," she said, and suddenly her eyes widened. At the same time Denise realized why—and her mouth fell open. They had on identical T-shirts—with "I love L.A." emblazoned across them!

Britt started laughing. "I thought I was the only one in town who had this shirt! My cousin in Los Angeles sent it to me. Where did you get yours?"

Denise smiled modestly. "I got it in L.A. last year when I was visiting my aunt."

"Wow!" Britt exclaimed. "You've actually *been* to Los Angeles! What was it like?"

All Denise had time to say was "Fantastic." The teacher, Ms. Cooper, was calling for their attention.

As Ms. Cooper passed out the tests, Denise basked in the glow of the brief exchange she had had with Britt. It was no big deal as far as conversations went, but it had brought back a rush of memories of silly, casual conversations with girlfriends back home. Now, more than ever, she longed to be part of a group here at Lakeside.

Silently she rebuked herself. *Don't be silly, you've got Pete, and you don't need anyone else*. But for some reason she wasn't convinced.

She was almost glad they were having a test, so she could concentrate on it rather than her worrisome thoughts. Denise didn't find the test difficult. That was one benefit of not having any friends, she reflected. She had plenty of time to study!

After Ms. Cooper had gathered the papers, she perched on the edge of her desk and addressed the class. "As I told you at the beginning of the term, you're required to give an oral presentation in this class. Since there are twenty-four students, I'm afraid we don't have enough class time for each of you to give an individual presentation."

"Gee, that's too bad," one guy said in mock dismay.

Ms. Cooper's eyes twinkled. "You're not getting off *that* easily! We *do* have enough time to hear twelve reports. So I'm asking you to choose a partner, select a topic, and give your presentations in groups of two."

Denise felt sick. Who would want to team up with her? A boy raised his hand.

"What kind of topics are we supposed to choose?"

Mrs. Cooper smiled. "I think you should all have a good time preparing these presentations. I want you to explore some aspect of popular culture, something you're really interested in. For example, you might want to investigate the appeal of soap operas."

"Wow!" one girl exclaimed. "You mean we can give a report on 'Ryan's Hope'?"

"Sure," Ms. Cooper replied. "But you can't just get up here and tell us what the show is about. You need to look at it in a different way. What sort of values does that particular soap opera promote? What kinds of messages are presented? You'll have to ask yourselves a lot of questions. Here's another possible topic—the punk movement. What does that mean in terms of fashion, music, and life-style?"

By now the class was buzzing excitedly. A germ of an idea had begun to grow in Denise's mind—and the more she thought about it, the better it seemed.

The bell rang, and Ms. Cooper hopped off her desk. "I'll want to know your topics by Monday," she called out as the students gathered up their books and began to file out noisily.

"I can't think of anything. Can you?"

Denise turned and looked at Britt, who had a worried look on her face.

"I do have an idea," she admitted. "But I'm not sure if it will work."

"What is it?" Britt asked eagerly.

"I was thinking about music videos,"

Denise said. Before she could say any more, Britt's eyes lit up, and she clapped her hands together.

"What a great idea!" she exclaimed. "Hey, do you have someone you'll ask to work with you?"

Denise shook her head. "Would you like to work with me?" she asked hesitantly.

"You got it!" Britt said. "It sounds like fun! My folks have a video cassette recorder. We could tape some examples of videos and have a really classy presentation."

The next class was beginning to come into the room.

"I have to run," Britt said. "What's your phone number?"

Denise scribbled it down and gave it to her.

"I'll call you tonight, and we can get together on this," Britt called as she dashed from the room.

Going into her last class, Denise felt better than she had in ages—almost as good as she had when she first started going out with Pete. Maybe now she had a chance to make a friend at Lakeside and maybe, through Britt, she'd get to know some other kids at school.

She daydreamed all through class. *I probably could have made friends with Britt months ago—if only I weren't so shy! I've just got to come out of this shell I'm in and stop being so afraid of people. Britt Leland is one of the most popular girls at school, and she has actually been friendly to me!*

She left the class with a sense of having set a new goal for herself. Quickly she went to her locker, pulled out her jacket, and ran around the corner to meet Pete at his locker.

She had to suppress a giggle when she thought about that locker. Some people met on the beach, or in a park, or at a restaurant—and then it became *their* restaurant or beach or park. How could a person get romantic about a locker?

But he was waiting for her—there at the spot where they had first met—at *their* locker. And she felt that special thrill, that familiar tingle, that she always felt whenever she saw him.

"Hi," she said happily. Pete smiled as he took a couple of books from the locker and added them to the already heavy load in his arms.

"Wow, you must have a lot of homework," she commented as they strolled down the hall toward the exit.

"Not really," Pete replied. "These are computer books I got from the library. I want to try some new programs. How was your day?"

"Good," Denise said. "We've got a really

great assignment in sociology." She proceeded to tell him about her music video idea.

"That sounds like fun," Pete said. "Just think—you get to watch music videos for homework!"

Denise giggled. "I can't wait till my parents yell at me to turn off MTV." She made an exaggeratedly innocent expression. "But, Mom, I *have* to watch videos. It's for school!"

Pete laughed. "You can tell them you've decided to major in New Wave!"

"Britt Leland's going to be working with me on the project," Denise continued. "Do you know her?"

"Not really," Pete said. "I mean, I know who she *is*. She's the leader of the jet set." That was what Pete always called the popular group.

Something about his tone made Denise feel defensive. "I think she's nice," she said.

Pete shrugged. "Maybe. But those kids she runs around with—"

"Do they have bad reputations?" Denise asked curiously.

Pete shook his head. "Not that I know of. I just don't understand why kids have to herd together, like sheep. They act alike, they dress alike—"

"Hey, look!" Denise interrupted, pointing to a sign on the school door. It announced that a new computer club was forming.

"Tuesday, three-thirty, room one-seven-teen," she read aloud, and turned to Pete. "Are you going to go?"

Pete made a face. "No, I'm not into clubs. Once you join a club, you have to go to meetings and see people—anyway, I like to work alone." He paused and smiled at Denise affectionately. "Besides," he added, "the less time I spend with other people, the more time I get to spend with you."

Denise smiled back at him. "Now, that's what I call a good excuse."

Chapter Two

"Mom?"

"In here!"

Denise and Pete followed the voice coming from the kitchen, where Denise's mother was sitting at the table. Her head was cocked to one side, and she was holding the phone receiver on her shoulder. With one hand she was taking notes, with the other she was fumbling through a card file. She flashed a welcoming smile at the two of them, pointed to the refrigerator, then spoke into the phone.

"That's right, Mrs. Hearne," she said in a businesslike voice. "I can get both lamps in beige, and I think they'll go perfectly with the Oriental rug."

Denise went to the refrigerator and pulled out a bakery box, which she set on the table. "Yum, pound cake," she said when she had opened the box. Meanwhile, Pete gathered plates, napkins, and forks. It was a familiar routine for them. Pete came home with her almost every day, and sometimes he stayed for dinner.

Denise could understand why he might not want to go straight home. Usually, the only person there was the housekeeper. Pete's mother had died a few years before, his father traveled a lot on business, and he didn't have any brothers or sisters.

Mrs. Taylor hung up the phone, then turned to Denise and Pete. "One more call, kids, and then I'll join you." Quickly she dialed a number.

"Martha? I can come look at the master bedroom on Thursday." She paused, listening, and then said, "Great. We'll have lunch and talk about your ideas."

As she cut slices from the pound cake and poured milk for Pete and herself, Denise watched her mother with admiration. She was an interior decorator, and she had wasted no time in drumming up business in the community.

"Well, you guys, how goes it?" she asked as she replaced the phone.

"Fine, Mom," Denise replied, sitting down at the table. "Want some cake?"

Her mother grimaced. "I'd love some, but

I'm going to be good and say no. Unfortunately, sweetie, I don't have your svelte figure. I'll just have some black coffee."

"How's business, Mrs. Taylor?" Pete asked as Denise's mother poured herself a cup of coffee from the coffeemaker that stood on the counter.

She brightened. "Fantastic! In the city there was too much competition. This town is perfect for me."

Denise was glad to hear Lakeside was perfect for someone.

As Mrs. Taylor joined Pete and Denise at the table, she handed her daughter an opened envelope.

"A letter from Courtney!" Denise exclaimed in delight, pulling it out of the envelope and quickly scanning it.

Her mother nodded. "I can't believe she actually found time to write. With all her dashing around at college, it sounds as though she never stands still." She shook her head with amusement. "I just hope her studies don't interfere with her social life."

Denise envisioned her vivacious older sister—pretty, popular, and always high-spirited.

"I miss her," she said wistfully. "Wait till you meet Courtney, Pete. She's off the scale."

"She can't be any more off the scale than her

sister," he replied loyally, and Denise smiled at him.

"She'll be home for her spring break," Mrs. Taylor said, then glanced at the wall clock. "Wow, it's getting late. I've got to pick up something at an antique shop. Pete, are you staying for dinner?"

Pete grinned. "Thanks, but not tonight, Mrs. Taylor. My father's coming home."

"How nice," she said. Then she added, "Not that you're not always welcome here. See you kids later."

After she left the kitchen, Pete turned to Denise, and his face was troubled. "Sometimes I think I hang out here too much," he said slowly. "Do you think your parents mind?"

"Don't be silly," Denise said briskly, finishing her piece of cake. "They like me to bring people home. Back in the city, Courtney always filled the apartment with her friends. Besides," Denise added, "Mom thinks it must be lonely for you at home with your father gone so much."

Pete shrugged. "It's not so bad," he said. "I kind of like having the house to myself." Then he reached out and gently touched her cheek. "Anyway, that's *not* why I hang out here, and you know it."

After clearing the plates from the table,

Denise and Pete went into the den, where Denise turned on the television. There was a wilderness movie on, which Pete wanted to see, and they settled back on the sofa. The movie looked boring to Denise. But Pete became engrossed in it, so Denise pulled out Courtney's letter and started to reread it, slowly this time.

Her sister was obviously having a ball at college. The letter was packed with vivid detail—about new friends, dates, the drama club.

"She's having a terrific time," she told Pete when a commercial came on, and she read him part of the letter.

"Spring Frolic was unreal! All the sororities put on crazy skits, and afterward there was a fantastic concert in the gym. Later, Sam took me to his fraternity house for a party. We danced till way past midnight!"

"She likes to party, doesn't she?"

"Definitely," Denise replied. "Courtney's very sociable. She likes having lots of people around." Even as she spoke, she knew there was a note of envy in her voice. Pete looked at her curiously.

"You're not jealous, are you?"

Denise shook her head. "No—not really. Well, maybe a little. Courtney's always had such an easy time meeting people. I don't think I could be like her—even if I tried."

"Don't try," Pete said. "I love you just the way you are."

Denise gave him a quick kiss. Deep in her heart, she knew she didn't want to be Courtney. Courtney didn't have Pete.

The commercial was over, and the movie came on again.

"What's this about?" Denise asked, indicating the screen.

"It's kind of cool," Pete said. "This guy and his wife have left everything behind to live alone in the hills. They're trying to get back to nature, or something like that. Anyway, there isn't another person around for miles."

"Sounds lonely," Denise remarked.

"I don't think so," Pete said. "I mean, if you're with the person you love, why do you need anyone else?"

For some reason his answer bothered her, but she didn't say anything. They watched the movie in silence, and when it was over, Pete checked his watch.

"I'd better get going. My father should be home pretty soon." Denise walked him to the door.

"I'll call you later," he promised, and they

kissed lightly. As she watched him walk away, her mother's car pulled up.

"Denise? Could you come help me with this?" her mother called as she stepped out of the station wagon. Denise ran out to the car and helped her lift a large, carved wooden object from the back of the car.

"What *is* it?"

"It's a headboard," her mother replied, laughing. "You know, for a bed. Pretty gruesome, huh?"

Between the two of them, they managed to lug the mammoth slab of oak into the house.

"Why are we bringing it in here?"

They gently lowered it to the floor, and Mrs. Taylor sighed in relief. "There! What did you say, Denise?"

"How come we brought it inside instead of leaving it in the car? I assume it's not for *your* bed—and I hope it's not for mine!"

Her mother laughed. "Don't worry about that. I just want to polish it up a little before my client sees it." She shook her head as she gazed at the ugly headboard. "Martha Leland is a lovely person, but her taste in furniture— yuck!"

Denise blinked. "Did you say Leland?"

"Mmmm." Her mother nodded as she moved toward the kitchen. "She's a new client of mine. I think she has a daughter about your age."

"I know," Denise said, following her. "She's in my sociology class."

"I met her once or twice," her mother said. "But I can't remember her name."

"Britt," Denise offered. "She's one of the most popular girls at Lakeside High."

"Really?" Mrs. Taylor went to the refrigerator and took out a large steak. "She seems like a nice girl."

"She is," Denise said. "In fact, she's going to be my partner for our sociology project."

There was no mistaking the tone of pleasure in her mother's voice. "Oh, Denise, I'm so glad you're starting to make some friends."

Denise grimaced. "Come on, Mom, it's no big deal. I hardly even know her." She paused, then added, "But you're right. It would be nice to have some friends again."

"You will," her mother promised. "You just need to leave yourself open to friendship and not cut yourself off from people." She hesitated, then said gently, "It might help if you weren't with Pete so much of the time."

"Mom! I thought you liked Pete!"

"Oh, I do," her mother replied hastily as she seasoned the steak. "I think he's a fine boy. But you two are together constantly. You don't seem to have time for any other friends."

"Maybe I don't need any other friends," Denise said stiffly. "I'm perfectly happy being with Pete."

"Honey, everyone needs friends," her mother persisted. "Your father and I are perfectly happy together, too, but we also have friends we see."

"Pete doesn't think it's important to have other people around," Denise said. "He says all we need is each other."

Mrs. Taylor frowned. "Maybe Pete needs to come out of his shell a little bit, too. When he's not with you, he's home and usually alone—"

"But Pete *likes* to be alone, Mom," Denise objected.

Her mother raised her eyebrows. "That's what he *says*," she noted, giving Denise a significant look. "But do you know how Pete really feels about being alone?"

Denise stared at her mother. She had to admit that she'd often asked herself that same question. Did Pete honestly enjoy being alone so much of the time? Or was he just too proud to admit that he might ever feel lonely?

But for some reason she didn't want to let her mother think that she might be right about Pete. Pete was her boyfriend, and Denise didn't want to sound disloyal to him.

"Pete is absolutely perfect, just the way he is," she stated firmly. As she heard the door slam and her father's hearty "I'm home!" she secretly sighed in relief. *Maybe that will put an end to this conversation*, she thought.

But no such luck.

"Good evening, lovely wife and charming daughter," Mr. Taylor greeted them jovially as he joined them in the kitchen. Then he looked around the room with a perplexed expression, as if something were missing.

"No Pete?"

Denise felt her face go red. "Aw, come on, Dad, don't you get on my case, too."

Her father looked completely innocent. "What did I say?"

Denise sighed. "Sorry, Dad. I just thought you were going to say something about Pete hanging around all the time. Mom thinks Pete and I are together too much."

"Now, Denise, that's not what I said," her mother objected. "I just think you might want to have some other people around once in a while, too."

Denise managed a smile. "I know, Mom. You're right. And I *am* going to try to get to know some other kids. It's just not that easy."

But I will try, she thought as she helped her mother fix dinner. Much as she loved Pete, much as she loved being with him, she *did* want to have more friends at Lakeside. Not boyfriends, of course, just—friends. She remembered her resolution earlier in the day in class, and she made a mental note to keep it. She would make new friends, and they'd be Pete's friends, too. Her mother was right— Pete did need to come out of his shell.

The phone rang after dinner, just as she was clearing the table. "I'll get it," Denise called out. "It's probably Pete." She walked over to the kitchen wall phone and picked up the receiver. "Hello?"

"Hi, Denise? It's me, Britt Leland."

"Oh! Hi, Britt."

"Listen," Britt said, "the more I think about your music video idea, the more I love it. Can you come over tomorrow after school so we can talk about it?"

"Sure," Denise said.

"Great! I'll meet you by the main door after our last class. Bye!"

Her mother came into the kitchen just as Denise was hanging up the phone. "Was that Pete?"

"No," Denise said. "It was Britt Leland. She wants me to come over after school tomorrow so we can work on that class project."

"Terrific!" her mother said happily. "See! I told you you'd start making friends."

Denise found her mother's obvious enthusiasm a little overwhelming, but she had to admit to herself that she was pretty pleased, too. But before she could say anything, the phone rang again.

"Denise? Hi, it's me." Pete's voice sounded strangely subdued.

"Hi! Did you and your dad go out to dinner?"

"No," Pete said slowly. "He called. He had another meeting, and he won't be home till tomorrow."

"Oh. What did you do for dinner?"

"Mrs. Grimes fixed me something."

Denise pictured the silent, grim-looking housekeeper handing Pete a plateful of dinner, which he would eat in solitude.

"You should have come over," she said softly.

"That's OK," Pete said. "You know I don't mind being alone. And, besides, it gave me a chance to look at those computer books." His voice brightened. "I've been playing around with a program, and I think I've actually designed a terrific new game!"

"All right!" Denise exclaimed. She didn't really share Pete's passion for computers and video games, but she always tried to sound as enthusiastic as she could.

"We can try it out tomorrow after school," he said.

"OK," Denise said, and then she caught herself and said, "No—wait, I can't. I'm going over to Britt Leland's tomorrow to work on our sociology project."

There was a silence on the other end of the line.

"Pete? Are you there?"

"Yeah, I'm here. Look, I've got homework to do. I'll talk to you tomorrow, OK?"

"Sure." As she hung up the phone, her forehead wrinkled. Pete sounded strange—almost annoyed. Why should he care if she worked on a project with Britt?

He was probably just feeling lonely, she decided. No mother, his father away from home, and now his girlfriend was temporarily deserting him. Again, she resolved to make a real effort to bring other people into their lives. She'd see to it that Pete wouldn't be lonely anymore.

Chapter Three

As usual the school cafeteria was crowded and noisy. Denise gripped her tray with both hands as she edged her way through the roomful of kids to the table where Pete was waiting. She saw him before he saw her, and his expression was glum. It reminded her of the tone in his voice on the telephone the night before.

"Pete?"

When he saw her, his eyes lit up, and she felt relieved.

"Hi, beautiful."

Denise felt warm all over. She knew that her hair was a mess, but when Pete called her beautiful, she *felt* beautiful.

"You looked so miserable a second ago when I was walking up," she said, putting her tray down on the table and sitting down across from him. "Is something wrong?"

Pete grinned and indicated the tray in front of him. "I was just trying to decide whether or not I was hungry enough to risk my life and actually eat this stuff."

Denise looked down at the unidentifiable brown mass on her own tray and nodded understandingly.

"They should have a daily contest. Try to guess what's on your tray, and win—"

"A gift certificate to McDonald's," Pete finished.

"Well, at least we know what these are," Denise said as she put her fork into the mound of peas nestling next to the brown stuff.

"Don't be too sure," Pete warned her. "That could be corn they've dyed green."

Denise took a bite. "You may be right. We'd better stop talking about the food, or I'll lose my appetite altogether. Tell me about your new computer game."

"I can't describe it," Pete said. "But wait till you play it! I swear it's as good as any game I've ever played in an arcade."

"I once read an article about a guy who invented a game, and he made a million dollars," Denise said, taking a sip of milk.

"Wouldn't that be something," Pete murmured. "If I had a million dollars—"

"What would you do with it?" Denise asked curiously.

A dreamy expression came over his face, and he set down his fork. "If I had a million dollars," he said slowly, "I'd build a house on a mountain, miles away from anyone else. Just for you and me."

Denise smiled, but his words bothered her a little. Pete was always talking like that, and there was something troubling about it. Her eyes drifted to a table nearby where half a dozen kids were talking and laughing. They looked as though they were having fun.

"Hi, Denise!"

Britt Leland waved to her from beside the conveyor belt on which she was putting her empty tray. Denise waved back, and Britt mouthed "See you later" as she moved toward the exit.

When Denise looked back at Pete, she couldn't help noticing that he looked glum again.

"Britt and I are going to start working on our project this afternoon," she said, taking a bite of the brown mass, which had turned out to be stew.

Pete nodded. "Yeah, you told me about that." He paused, then added, "I once had to work with a partner on a class project. It was the pits. He was really lazy, and I ended up doing all the work for both of us."

"I don't think Britt will be like that," Denise objected. "She acted so excited about my idea."

Pete shrugged. "You never know. But those kids she hangs out with are not exactly famous for their scholastic achievement."

Again his remarks troubled her. She could tell he was upset about something, and she had a feeling there was more to it than her working on a school project with Britt.

"Pete," she began gently. "What's bugging you? Why are you so upset about my working with Britt?"

Pete didn't answer immediately. He swirled the remaining milk in his glass and looked strangely uncomfortable, as if he didn't know exactly how to say what he wanted to say. Then he drank down the rest of the milk and said slowly, "I'm not bent out of shape about your working with Britt. It's just that—well, I guess—in a way—I'm afraid of losing you."

Denise was perplexed. "How could you lose me to Britt? Maybe you haven't noticed this, Pete, but she's a girl."

Pete managed a smile. "Hey, thanks for telling me." Then he got serious again. "That's not what I'm worried about. I just keep thinking that if you get in with Britt and her crowd, you'll fall for some Mister-Cool type. You know, like one of those jet-set guys."

"Oh, Pete," Denise said and rolled her eyes toward the ceiling. "Give me a break. How could you even imagine a dumb thing like that?" She glanced around the room and lowered her voice. The Lakeside cafeteria wasn't exactly the perfect place for romantic declarations. "Pete, I love you."

She waited for that to sink in before she continued. "But I'd still like to make some friends. *Girl*friends. I may be shy, but I'm not the totally committed loner that you are."

Pete looked as though he wanted to say something, but then he didn't, so Denise went on. "Just because I want to meet some new people doesn't mean I want to *date* new people."

When she finished, she took a deep breath. She felt as though she had just given a speech! She knew her voice was convincing, because every word she had said was true. She had absolutely no desire to go out with anyone else, and she couldn't imagine ever having feelings for another boy like the ones she had for Pete.

Pete was looking a little sheepish—as well he should for having doubted her, she thought. A faint suggestion of a smile appeared on his good-looking face.

"I know," he said softly. "I'm being dumb. And selfish. You should have friends. Just because I'm such a hermit doesn't mean you have to be one, too."

They were both silent then, but their eyes communicated. Then Denise noticed the time.

"I'd better run, or I'll be late for class," she murmured, reluctant to break the magical silence. They both rose slowly, gathered their trays and books, and left the table.

"What time is your father coming home?" she asked as they placed their trays on the conveyor belt and moved toward the exit.

"Not till late," Pete said.

"Then come for dinner," Denise urged. "I'm sure I'll be home from Britt's about five-thirty."

Pete agreed, and they parted at the door. As she made her way to P.E., Denise thought about Pete's father. She'd only met him a few times. He was always polite and pleasant, but he seemed unusually quiet, even remote. Pete had once told her that his father had never really recovered from his mother's death and that he had thrown himself into his work as a way of keeping busy all the time. Which left Pete pretty much on his own—and alone. But not completely alone, of course. He had Denise, and Denise knew she'd always be there for him.

It seemed strange not to be meeting him after school that day. In fact, when she left her locker, she automatically began walking toward "their" locker. Then she remembered Britt.

Britt was waiting outside the main door of the school. She wasn't alone. Two other girls were standing with her. One of them looked sort of familiar. Denise approached them hesitantly, but Britt greeted her with enthusiasm.

"Hi! Do you know Susan and Ingrid?"

Susan, a sweet-looking girl with short, wavy blond hair, smiled and said, "Hi." The other one, a tall girl with flaming red hair, just nodded. Suddenly Denise remembered where she had seen her before—in the locker room after P.E. She was the one who had just broken up with someone named Billy.

Denise murmured something like "Glad to meet you." And then Susan turned to Ingrid.

"We'd better get going if we're going to change clothes for the tryouts. Britt, I'll call you later. Nice meeting you, Denise."

Ingrid languidly shifted her books to her other arm. "Yeah, see you, Britt." Her eyes rested briefly on Denise, and she muttered,

"Bye" before following Susan back inside the building.

"What sort of tryouts are they going to?" Denise asked curiously as she and Britt walked down the steps.

"Cheerleading," Britt explained. "Every year they have new tryouts. Even the old cheerleaders have to try out for the next year's squad."

Then, rather abruptly, she changed the subject. "How do you like sociology?"

"I kind of like it," Denise said. "It's a lot of work, but it's pretty interesting. And Ms. Cooper seems like a good teacher."

"So far, I've only gotten B's in that class," Britt said. "And I really need to get an A. How are you doing?"

Denise admitted that Ms. Cooper had given her mostly A's on all the tests and papers.

"Wow," Britt said respectfully. "Cooper's one of the toughest teachers at Lakeside. You must really be smart."

Denise just shrugged. She didn't want Britt to know that she got A's because she had so much time on her hands to study.

It didn't take them long to walk to Britt's house. On the outside it looked pretty much like the others on that block—a two-story, white clapboard, set back on a manicured lawn. Inside, though, it was something else altogether. Even though Denise remembered what her mother had said about Mrs. Leland's taste, she wasn't at all prepared for the elaborate decor of the rooms. It seemed as though everything in the house—from the furniture to the frames around the paintings—was an ostentatiously carved, Victorian antique.

Denise hoped the expression on her face didn't reveal her reaction, but she had the feeling that she wasn't very successful. Britt gave her an amused look.

"Pretty awful, huh? My mother's got great taste in clothes, but her choice in furniture leaves something to be desired. Let's go get something to eat, and then we can go up to my room."

After eating one of Britt's specialties— frozen pizza fixed up with anything in the fridge—they went to Britt's room, which showed none of her mother's influence. If anything, it represented the opposite of what Denise had seen downstairs. Everything was sleek, modern, and functional, but the bright colors kept it from looking dull.

"This is nice," Denise said with admiration.

"I decorated it myself," Britt said proudly. "My mother hates it! I'll bet you've got a nice house. Your mother's an interior decorator, isn't she?"

Denise nodded. "She's got excellent taste in

furniture. But her taste in clothes is terrible! You should see the stuff she brings home for me sometimes. Honestly, I swear she must think I'm still ten years old."

"I know what you mean." Britt groaned as she flopped down on one of her twin beds. Denise sat down on the other bed and looked at the framed photographs that rested on the small nightstand between the beds. In one photo Britt was posed in a Lakeside cheerleading outfit.

"I was a cheerleader last year and first semester this year," Britt said.

"How come you're not on the squad now?"

Britt looked a little embarrassed. "My grades. They went down last term, and my parents blamed cheerleading. Actually, they think it's a combination of cheerleading and Mick." She smiled gently and indicated another photo on the nightstand. "Mick's the guy I go with."

Denise thought she recognized the sullen-looking, but attractive, boy she had seen Britt with at school several times.

"You go with Pete Carruthers, don't you?"

Denise nodded. "We've been going together for three months, ever since I moved here. Do you know him?"

"Not really," Britt said. "He was in one of my classes last term, but he never said much.

He's really cute, though." She paused and then said playfully, "Almost as much of a hunk as my Mick!"

Denise grinned, but secretly she thought Pete was a whole lot better looking than the thin, sort of scruffy-looking guy in the photo.

"To each her own," she said lightly.

Britt laughed. "Yeah, I guess everybody has different taste. My parents don't think Mick's good-looking at all." Her smile faded. "In fact, my parents don't think there's anything good about Mick. They've been down on him ever since we started going together."

"Why?"

Britt shrugged. "Who knows? I guess that's just the way parents are. Do your parents like Pete?"

"Sure," Denise said, then she remembered her conversation with her mother. "Well, they think I spend too much time with him."

"Oh, yeah, I get that all the time, too," Britt said. "I'm hoping that if I can get better grades, they'll quit nagging me about Mick." She made a face. "Right now, they only let me see him on weekends. He can't even come over on weekday nights!"

"That's awful," Denise said sympathetically. She couldn't imagine only being able to see Pete on weekends. "Well, at least you get to see him at school."

"Not that much," Britt said mournfully. "We don't have any classes together. And at lunchtime, he usually takes off with a couple of other guys. They go to some hamburger joint."

Denise was puzzled. "I thought it was against the rules to leave school at lunch."

Britt looked pained. "It is. And I keep asking Mick not to do it. He's going to get into big trouble one of these days." She smiled helplessly. "But I guess you just can't tell a guy like Mick what to do."

There was another photo on Britt's nightstand. It was a picture of Britt with her family.

"Is this your brother?" Denise asked, noticing a handsome young man standing behind Britt in the photo.

Britt groaned. "Sure is. And he's the bane of my existence." She laughed. "Actually, he's an OK guy. He's in college now. But he's always been so smart, so successful at everything he does, that compared with him I've always felt sort of—well—inferior, I guess." She shook her head. "I'm not blaming him. It's just that my parents are always throwing him up to me. You know—'Steven got straight A's. Steven was on the honor roll every year. Why can't you be more like Steven?' " She was doing a great imitation of a nagging voice, and Denise had to giggle. But then Britt sounded almost angry. "Why can't they understand that I'm not Steven? I'm just—me."

Denise nodded understandingly. "I have an older sister at college. She's always been so outgoing, dating lots of guys. Sometimes I wish I could be more like her. But at least my parents have never bugged me to be more like Courtney."

"You're lucky," Britt said.

The girls continued talking about their families and boyfriends for over an hour. Then suddenly Britt cocked her head to one side as if listening for something. "I think I hear my mother's car." She went over to the window and looked out. "Yep. Here comes the queen of the nagging mothers. Just wait. In thirty seconds she'll be up here checking on me to see if my nose is buried in my homework."

Sure enough, a few seconds later Denise could hear footsteps on the stairs. She waited apprehensively to catch a glimpse of this ogre Britt had described.

To her surprise, the woman who appeared at the bedroom door had a friendly, mild-mannered expression on her strikingly attractive face. Like Britt, Mrs. Leland was blond and slender. She looked very chic in a tailored suit.

"Hi, Mom," Britt said in a voice that lacked much enthusiasm. "This is Denise Taylor."

"Hello, Denise," Mrs. Leland said warmly. "I know your mother. She's helping me redecorate the master bedroom."

A picture of that wretched ornate headboard flashed into Denise's mind, and she suppressed a giggle.

"Yes, I know," she said politely. "Pleased to meet you, Mrs. Leland."

"We're working together on a project for sociology," Britt said.

Mrs. Leland glanced at her watch. "Well, it's just about dinner time," she said pleasantly. "Denise, would you like to stay for dinner?"

"No, thanks, Mrs. Leland, I'm expected home. What time is it?"

"Just before six," Mrs. Leland said as she was leaving the room. "Well, do come another time."

Denise jumped up with a look of dismay. "My folks are going to kill me. I was supposed to be home by five-thirty." Another thought occurred to her. "And I told Pete to be there then!"

"And we haven't even talked about the project," Britt added. They stared at each other for a second, then burst out laughing.

"Well, at least we're getting to know each other," Britt said, and Denise agreed. She felt that they were on their way to becoming real friends.

"I've got an idea," Denise said. "On Sunday afternoon on MTV they're having the top ten videos. Why don't you come over to my place? We can watch the videos and jot down ideas for our project."

"OK," Britt said. "Hey, I almost forgot to ask you. I'm having a party Saturday night. No big deal, just a get-together. Can you and Pete come?"

Denise felt a rush of pleasure. This was what she had been hoping for—a chance to get to know some of the kids from school.

"I'll ask Pete," she said. "But I'm sure it'll be OK."

She practically ran all the way home. There were so many thoughts racing through her head. She knew she'd be in trouble for being so late. At the same time she was exhilarated by the thought of the party on Saturday night. And she couldn't help being curious about Britt's tense relationship with her mother.

Sure enough, her mother was annoyed.

"Denise, we were getting worried about you," her mother said, frowning slightly. "I was just about to call the Lelands. And poor Pete's been here for over half an hour."

"I'm sorry, Mom," Denise said. "I guess I just lost track of the time. Where's Pete?"

"In the kitchen, setting the table," her mother said pointedly. Setting the table was Denise's job. Sometimes she felt as if she spent half her life putting dishes on the table and taking them off. But she managed to look appropriately apologetic, and the expression on her mother's face softened.

"Did you have a good time at Britt's?" she asked.

"Mom, we were working," she said, hoping the little fib didn't show on her face. "But Britt invited me to a party Saturday night."

Her mother looked pleased. "That's great! See, I told you you'd start making friends here."

Denise just hoped Pete would share her mother's enthusiasm. But she approached the kitchen with some doubts.

"Hi," she said. "Sorry I'm late."

At least Pete didn't look too irritated. "That's OK," he said. "I figure you're always worth waiting for." They both looked around, to make sure no one could see them, and quickly kissed.

"How was your meeting with Britt?"

"Well, we started talking and didn't get a whole lot of work done," Denise said as she started folding napkins. "Britt's having a party Saturday night, and she wants us to come."

She glanced at Pete, who seemed to be focusing on placing forks and knives on the table just so. His face was expressionless. At first she didn't think he had heard her. Then, quietly, he asked, "Do you want to go?"

"I wouldn't mind," she said casually. Then she figured she might as well be honest. "I do want to go, Pete. It would be a chance to get to know some of the kids at school."

"Yeah," Pete said unenthusiastically. "The thing is, my father will be home this weekend. I feel like I really should spend some time with him. And, well, you know, parties are really not my thing. But if you really want to go . . ."

Denise felt torn. She didn't want to force Pete to do something he didn't want to do. But on the other hand, she hated to pass up an opportunity like this.

"You do need some time with your father," she said slowly. "You know, Pete, I could go alone—"

Pete looked up eagerly. "Would you mind? Going alone?"

Denise knew she would mind—everyone else would probably have a date. But she forced herself to sound cheerful. "No, I don't mind."

Pete smiled at her gratefully. "You're wonderful," he said simply. Denise returned the smile. There was no way she could be annoyed with him. They drew closer, still smiling. And then they glanced around again, to make sure no one was looking.

Chapter Four

Early Saturday evening Denise's bedroom looked as though a tornado had struck it. Clothes from her closet were strewn all over. Sweaters and skirts lay on the bed, overalls, a jump suit, and three pairs of jeans were draped over a chair, and assorted shoes lay all around the floor. Denise stood in the center of the mess, pants in one hand, a skirt in the other, an expression of total panic on her face.

Britt had said it was just a casual get-together—but what did the kids at Lakeside *wear* to casual get-togethers? She looked over the jumble of clothes she'd been trying on and picked up her purple knit skirt and held it against a hot pink fluffy sweater. Cute—but if there was dancing, she'd get too hot.

Did kids at Lakeside dance at their parties?

Maybe the green overalls with a yellow shirt—no, that might be too casual.

"Denise! What a mess!" Her mother stood in the doorway, hands on her hips.

"I'll pick it all up," Denise quickly assured her.

"What's the problem?"

Glumly, Denise contemplated her clothes. "I don't know what to wear to Britt's."

Her mother briskly walked over to the almost empty closet and pulled out something Denise had stuffed way in the back.

"How about this sweet dress I bought you last year?" she asked brightly. Denise uttered a silent groan. "Sweet" described the dress perfectly. Pale yellow, with tucks leading down to a flowered belt and a full skirt. Perfect for Sunday school. Not perfect for a party.

But she didn't want to insult her mother. "It's a nice dress, Mom," she said carefully. "But I think this party is a little more, uh, casual. You know what I mean?" She knew she'd better make a decision quickly before her mother came up with another of her bright ideas.

"I'm going to wear my cropped jeans with a cotton sweater," she announced, realizing she was actually happy with her decision.

As she took a shower, dressed, and fussed with her hair, she thought about Pete. She wished he was going with her. But Britt had said it was perfectly OK to come alone, that lots of kids weren't bringing dates. Even so, she would miss not having him with her.

But she was glad he didn't mind her going to the party without him. Warmly she remembered his words when they had talked on the phone that very morning. "I know I've been selfish, Denise, trying to keep you all to myself. I love you, and I trust you, and I want you to have a good time and make lots of new friends. *Girl*friends," he added pointedly, and Denise had laughed. How could she ever even think about other boys when she had Pete?

Finally dressed and ready, she surveyed herself in the mirror. *Not bad*, she decided. Her short blond hair gleamed, the light blue sweater looked good against her fair skin, and the slim pants hugged her legs smoothly. A touch of pale blue eye shadow, a dab of pink gloss on her lips, and she was all ready. But ready for what? She was feeling almost as jittery as she had that first day at Lakeside. What if nobody talked to her? What if nobody liked her? She fixed her eyes firmly on her reflection in the mirror and gave herself a quick lecture. *Of course they'll talk to you—if you can overcome your silly shyness and talk to them.*

Shoulders back, head up, she marched into

the den to say good night to her parents. *Why did she feel like a soldier going off to do battle?*

"How are you getting to Britt's?" her mother asked.

"I'm going to walk," Denise replied. "It's only a few blocks away."

"But it's almost dark out," her father objected, rising from his armchair. "I'll drive you over."

"Oh, no, Dad, that's OK," Denise pleaded. "I don't mind walking." Was there anything more embarrassing than having your father drive you to a party? What if someone saw her?

"Well, I mind you walking," her father replied, and before Denise could say another word, he left the room to get the car keys.

Denise groaned audibly, and her mother gave her a sympathetic smile. "Tell him to let you off at the corner," she said with a conspiratorial wink.

Luckily her father didn't mind doing that, though Denise knew he'd be watching her from the car till she got into the house. As she approached the door, she could hear the faint sounds of rock music coming from the house. She took a deep breath, then pressed the door bell. Before she could even release the breath, Mrs. Leland opened the door.

"Hello, Denise," she said warmly. "Come on

in. The kids are all downstairs." She beckoned Denise to follow her. "I don't understand why Britt likes to entertain in the basement. It's so bare! I haven't even begun to decorate it." Denise stifled a giggle. Having seen Mrs. Leland's interior decorating, Denise knew one reason why Britt chose to have her parties in an empty basement!

As she went down the stairs, she was glad the music was so loud. At least no one could hear the sound of her heart pounding! She paused halfway down and surveyed the scene.

It was a large room. At one end, there was a long table with refreshments, and a bunch of kids were gathered there. Several couples were dancing in the middle of the room, and others were gathered in small groups. Some of the kids looked familiar, but she didn't see Britt. She recognized Susan, Britt's friend, whom she had met outside school a couple of days before. Susan smiled and waved.

"Denise, hi! Come on down!"

In the rush of introductions that followed, Denise found her nervousness fading.

"This is Lucy Kaplan, Jackie Rogers, Jim, Barry, and that's Neal over there." Denise tried to concentrate on remembering names, but it was hopeless. They all seemed nice, though, and she began to relax.

"Britt says you moved here from the city,"

one of the girls—was it Jackie?—said. "You must miss all the excitement."

"Sometimes," Denise admitted. "But it's nice to look out of my window and see an actual tree!"

"You're in my P.E. class, aren't you?" asked Lucy, a short, chubby girl in pink overalls. Denise wasn't sure. It was a big class, and in gymsuits everyone looked pretty much alike.

"Does it meet right after lunch?" she asked tentatively.

Lucy nodded. "How do you like Miss Bailey?" The mere mention of the husky, tough-looking gym teacher made Denise roll her eyes and make a face. Lucy nodded in agreement, and the two of them immediately began to share P.E. horror stories.

Just then Britt appeared. "Denise, I'm so glad you could come. Hey, I love your jeans!"

"Thanks," Denise said, and complimented Britt on her outfit, a cute purple miniskirt with a lavender sweater and matching tights.

"Denise is in my P.E. class," Lucy interjected. "We were just talking about that troll, Bailey."

Britt groaned. "I had her last year. She's terrible."

Susan was looking around the noisy room. "Where's Ingrid? Isn't she coming?"

"She'll be here," Britt said and grinned.

"You know how Ingrid likes to come to everything late and make an entrance."

A tall, slender boy came up behind Britt. Denise recognized him from the photo on Britt's nightstand. "Hey, come on, I want to dance," he muttered.

Britt turned to look up at him, and a dreamy smile crossed her face. "Mick, this is Denise," she said softly.

"Hi," Denise said. "I'm glad to meet you."

"Yeah," he said, looking totally uninterested. "Come on, let's dance."

He pulled Britt by the arm, away from the girls. Britt threw them a helpless smile and let herself be towed away. Jackie and Lucy drifted off, and Denise looked at Susan, who was shaking her head.

"He really pushes her around," she said. "I can't believe she puts up with it. Personally, I don't even know what she sees in him."

Denise had been wondering that, too. Mick was attractive and sort of sexy-looking. But the expression on his face was peculiar—insolent and sullen. And there was something about his small, beady eyes that kept him from being really good-looking.

"He's not very friendly, is he?" she remarked.

Susan sniffed. "That's the understatement of the year."

"I guess it's true what they say about 'opposites attract,' " Denise said. "I mean, Britt's so friendly and outgoing."

Susan nodded and sighed. "I worry that he might really hurt her one of these days." Then she brightened. "Hey, there's someone I want you to meet. He saw you come in, and I watched him watching you. He gave me a sign that he wants to meet you."

Denise followed her to the stereo, where a blond, broad-shouldered boy was standing alone, flipping through record albums.

"Denise Taylor, Billy Parrish," Susan said, introducing them. Billy smiled broadly.

"Hi! You must be new around here."

Denise felt her face getting pink. He was looking at her with obvious interest, and she was afraid that if she looked directly into his eyes she'd go completely scarlet.

"Uh, sort of," she said. "I mean, I just moved to Lakeside three months ago."

"You're kidding!" Billy exclaimed and turned to Susan. "How could a girl this cute have been around for three months and I haven't noticed her?"

The exaggerated shock in his voice made Denise laugh. Susan laughed, too. "Well, for the past few months you've only had eyes for one girl, Billy."

Now it was Billy's turn to get a little pink.

"Hey, that's all over, and you know it," he said and turned back to Denise. "I'm a free man now."

Denise didn't know what they were talking about, but she was definitely aware of one thing—Billy was flirting with her! Strangely enough, she didn't feel uncomfortable about that. In fact, it felt good!

Susan gave her a meaningful look. "I think I'll let you two get acquainted," she said, and with a wink she left them there.

Billy grinned. "Smart girl. She knows when to leave."

Denise gulped. This guy got right to the point! Frantically she tried to think of something to say. She indicated the album he was holding. "Do you like Rod Stewart?"

Billy shrugged. "He's OK. This album's good for dancing. How about it?"

"How about what?"

He rolled his eyes. "Dancing!"

"Oh!" She looked up at him. His eyes were incredibly blue.

"Hey, Parrish." A large, husky boy in a Lakeside football jacket approached them. "I was talking to Coach Hudson on Friday. He says Riverside's got a new quarterback who's going to be hard to stop next year."

"Oh, yeah? Who is it?"

As the two boys talked football, Denise

wasn't sure what to do. Did Billy still want to dance with her? She realized she hadn't danced in ages. Would she make a fool of herself? Pete wasn't much into dancing, and, of course, they hadn't been to any parties.

Thinking of Pete made her feel a little guilty. She wondered if she should mention him. Billy might be a "free man," but Denise knew she was definitely *not* a "free woman." On the other hand, Billy was probably just the type who flirted with all the girls. It didn't mean anything. And surely Pete wouldn't mind if she just danced with the guy. He'd *want* her to have a good time, wouldn't he?

"Sorry about the interruption." Billy's voice was apologetic. "Now, how about the dance?"

Denise mentally assured herself again that Pete wouldn't care and smiled brightly. "OK."

Chapter Five

Denise had almost forgotten how much she loved to dance, and Billy was a good dancer. He moved easily and comfortably, not like some guys who looked so awkward on the dance floor—like Mick, who was dancing with Britt right next to them. Actually he didn't even look as if he were dancing—he just shrugged his shoulders to the beat of the music. He barely looked at Britt. His eyes were darting around the room, and he seemed restless and bored. Britt obviously didn't care, though. She was smiling and looking up at him with a dreamy expression on her face.

Billy certainly didn't look bored. His smile was so infectious that Denise found herself smiling back at him easily. He really was very good-looking, with his athletic build, fair hair, and blue eyes. Not as good-looking as

Pete, Denise thought loyally—but definitely cute.

When the song ended, he said, "Hey, you're a great dancer! Let's do it again." But before Denise could reply, a voice broke in from behind her.

"Hello, Billy."

Denise could see Billy's expression change before she turned around to see who was speaking. It was as if a curtain had fallen over his face.

"Hi, Ingrid," he said stiffly.

The tall redhead totally ignored Denise as she moved closer to Billy. "I just got here," she said languidly. "What have you been up to?" The question was simple enough, but there was something insinuating in the way she asked it.

Billy coughed. "Uh, do you know Denise?"

Ingrid's gaze rested on Denise, and Denise began to feel distinctly uncomfortable. There was a coldness in her eyes that made Denise imagine that Ingrid was trying to tell her something—something not very nice.

"Yeah," Ingrid said and then turned back to Billy. "I'm absolutely dying to dance," she murmured.

"Uh—Denise and I were just getting something to drink," Billy replied quickly. He took

Denise firmly by the hand and pulled her toward the refreshment table.

Lucy and Susan were there, and Susan grinned mischievously at Billy. "Better watch out, Billy. Ingrid's made her entrance,"

"I know," Billy muttered. "I saw her. Denise, you want some punch?"

"Sure," Denise replied, trying to figure out what was going on between Billy and Ingrid. Suddenly something clicked in her mind. She remembered that conversation she had overheard in the locker room. Hadn't Ingrid said she had just broken up with someone named Billy?

Several other kids gathered at the table, and Billy introduced her to them. The names flew by so quickly Denise barely had time to attach names to faces. Was the wiry boy with the copper-colored hair Jim, and the guy with the glasses Jerry? Or was it the other way around? No matter, she decided—she'd learn all their names eventually. They were all acting so friendly, and a sense of warmth filled her as she realized that she was actually beginning to feel comfortable, as if she could really feel at home in Lakeside.

Britt and Mick joined them. "Having a good time?" Britt asked her a little anxiously. "I know I should be looking out for you more, but"—she lowered her voice—"Mick gets so possessive, you know what I mean?"

"I'm having a great time," Denise assured her. "I'm really glad you invited me."

"Don't worry about Denise," Billy interjected and tossed an arm carelessly around her shoulders. "I'm watching out for her."

Britt's eyes widened as she looked from Denise to Billy, and Denise had a sinking feeling in her stomach as she realized what Britt must be thinking.

She couldn't think of a way to get Billy's arm off her shoulders without seeming rude, but she knew she'd better say something quickly before Britt got the wrong idea.

"When I tell Pete about the party, I know he's going to be sorry he couldn't come," she said clearly. She wondered how Billy would react to this statement. To her dismay, he was engrossed in more football conversation with another boy and hadn't heard a word she said.

"I think I'll get some more punch," she said, letting Billy's arm slip off as she moved toward the punch bowl. Susan was ladling punch into cups and handed her one. Britt took one, too, and Susan turned to Mick.

"Want some punch?"

Mick glanced at the cup Susan was holding out to him.

"Nah," he said and pushed it away. Half of the punch spilled on Susan's pink skirt.

"Oh, no!" she exclaimed in dismay. Mick just glanced at her stained skirt, grunted something that sounded only vaguely like "sorry," and grabbed Britt's arm.

"Let's dance," he said, pulling her away.

Susan looked forlorn. "My favorite skirt," she moaned.

Denise looked at it. "It'll probably come out if you sponge it right away," she said. "Come on, I'll help you."

"Hey, where are you going?" Billy asked as Denise and Susan started toward the stairs.

"I'll be right back," Denise called over her shoulder.

"I think he likes you," Susan said as the two of them went upstairs to the bathroom.

"He seems like a nice guy," Denise replied. She wondered if she should tell Susan that she was already involved with someone. But that would sound as if she just assumed Billy was madly in love with her!

In the bathroom Susan slipped out of her skirt and began to dab at it with water and soap. The stain came out, but there was still a big wet spot. Susan groaned.

"Now what am I going to do? I can't go down there in a soaking wet skirt!"

Denise spotted a blow dryer hanging on the

wall. "I've got an idea!" Susan held the skirt up while Denise turned on the dryer and directed the stream of air at the wet spot.

"Hey, it's drying," Susan said. "Denise, you are absolutely brilliant!"

As Denise waved the dryer back and forth across the skirt, Susan told her about Billy and Ingrid.

"See, they were going out for a few weeks, and then Ingrid got tired of him. That's what she's like—she goes after a guy, then once she's got him, she doesn't want him anymore."

"How weird," Denise remarked. "Doesn't she ever fall in love with anybody?"

Susan made a face. "The only person Ingrid loves is Ingrid. Anyway, she broke up with Billy and started chasing some senior, but I guess he wasn't interested. So now she wants Billy back, but I'm pretty sure she's not going to get him this time."

"Why?"

Susan gave Denise an exasperated look. "Oh, come on, Denise, I saw how Billy's been looking at you all night! He's definitely interested."

Denise smiled weakly. "Do you really think so?"

"Absolutely," Susan replied. "But beware of Ingrid! Once she knows she's got competition—"

Denise interrupted her. "Well, Ingrid doesn't have to worry about me. Billy seems really cool, but—well, I'm pretty much involved with someone else."

"Who?"

"Pete Carruthers."

Susan's forehead wrinkled. "Who's he? Does he go to Lakeside?"

Mentally Denise scolded Pete for not having come to the party with her. "He's new in town, too," she explained. "And he's kind of a loner, but he's wonderful when you get to know him. I've been going out with him for three months."

"Why didn't he come with you tonight?"

Denise didn't want to go into the whole story. "He already had plans," she said evasively. "But, anyway, the point is that I'm not really interested in going out with anyone else."

Susan looked thoughtful, as if she were trying to decide whether or not to tell Denise something.

"You know, Denise," she said slowly, "you're new here, and you're just starting to get to know people. Billy's really popular, and it wouldn't hurt you to go out with him."

Denise shook her head. "Seriously, Susan, I do want to get to know all these kids. But Pete and I have something pretty special together. And I think once people get to know him, they'll like him."

61

Susan grinned. "He must be special if you're going to pass up a chance to go out with Billy. He's really cute!"

"So's Pete," Denise assured her. "Believe me, once you meet him, you'll understand why I'm so loyal! There—I think your skirt's just about dry now."

"Hey, thanks a lot," Susan said as she put her skirt back on.

Billy was waiting for Denise at the bottom of the stairs when the girls returned to the party. "Well, it's about time," he said with mock impatience. "I was just about to ask someone else to dance!"

They danced to the next six records. Denise couldn't believe how much fun she was having. Occasionally she noticed Ingrid shooting menacing looks at her, but she managed to ignore her. Billy was incredibly attentive, Denise thought. When they weren't dancing, they were talking—or, at least, Billy was talking, mostly about the Lakeside football team. The conversation wasn't particularly enthralling, but Denise couldn't help being flattered by all his attention. Several times she thought she should tell him about Pete, but the moment never seemed quite right. She decided that if he ever got around to asking her out, she'd tell him then.

But for now, she was simply going to let herself have fun. It was so marvelous, being with all these kids, feeling almost as if she really belonged. It was exactly what she had been wishing for.

"Whew, it's getting warm in here," she gasped.

"Let's get some air," Billy suggested, indicating the sliding doors that led onto a terrace.

There was no one else on the terrace. It was a gorgeous evening—there were no clouds, the stars were bright, and a pretty quarter moon hung directly above them.

There was a slight chill in the air, and Denise involuntarily shivered.

"Cold?" Billy asked. She nodded. Billy murmured, "Me, too." And without any warning, he took her in his arms and kissed her.

Even as it was happening, she knew she should pull away. But she was feeling so exhilarated that it didn't seem wrong. And the kiss only lasted a second.

But as they separated, she came back down to earth. She knew she'd better tell him about Pete, right that minute. But before she could even open her mouth, a figure standing just inside the sliding doors caught her eye. Ingrid was watching them. And that peculiar smirk on her face suddenly made Denise feel very uneasy.

Chapter Six

On Sunday morning at ten o'clock Denise was still in bed and only half-awake. She lay there motionless, not yet willing to face the reality of the day. She wanted to hold on for just a few more minutes to her memories of the night before.

Billy had taken her home a full half hour past her curfew. Luckily her parents were so pleased that she was finally getting out and meeting people that they weren't angry with her.

She was glad that Billy had offered to take her home—even after she had told him about Pete. Her thoughts went back to the moment after they had kissed on the terrace. . . .

Seeing Ingrid standing there, watching them, brought her to her senses.

"I shouldn't have done that," she said.

Billy smiled. "Why not? It felt pretty good to me."

Denise glanced toward the terrace doors. Ingrid had disappeared. She took a deep breath.

"I'm sorry, Billy," she said hesitantly. "But, you see, I'm already going with someone."

"Oh, yeah?" Billy looked around quickly as if he expected to see some big hulking halfback appear out of nowhere and snatch Denise away.

"Pete Carruthers," Denise explained. "He couldn't come tonight."

Billy whistled softly. "If I had a girlfriend like you, I wouldn't let her go to parties alone." He grinned slyly. "She might meet some incredibly sexy football player and fall wildly in love."

Denise burst out laughing, and Billy pretended to be hurt.

"Seriously," she said when she got her voice under control, "Pete and I, well, we're pretty serious."

"I understand," Billy said easily. "Hey, so we kissed, no big deal."

"I didn't mean to lead you on," Denise said softly.

Billy shrugged. "It's not your fault. I was probably coming on too strong." Then he grinned and stuck out his right hand. "Friends?"

Denise took his hand and shook it firmly. "Friends." Then they both started laughing.

The rest of the evening passed pleasantly. Denise danced with Billy again, then with two other guys. It was an almost perfect evening, except for one strange moment with Ingrid.

The sultry redhead was eyeing her curiously over the punch bowl as Denise poured herself a cupful.

"I see you in the lunchroom all the time with the same guy—Pete something."

Denise smiled and tried to look friendly. "Pete Carruthers."

"Yeah," Ingrid said. "Cute guy. He's in my chem class. I've been meaning to introduce myself to him." Her half smile was more like a smirk. "I'll be *sure* to talk to him on Monday."

Her words seemed to carry a threat. What was she getting at? Denise wondered. Was she planning to flirt with Pete, to get even with Denise for kissing Billy? But Ingrid didn't say anything more. She just continued smiling in that odd way and walked away. What a weird girl. . . .

"Denise, want some breakfast?"

Her mother's voice pulled her out of her reverie, and Denise managed to drag herself out of bed.

"Thanks, I'm starving!" She pulled on a robe and followed her mother downstairs.

Her father was already digging into his scrambled eggs. "Well, here comes our sleeping beauty," he greeted her. "I guess you needed your sleep, considering what time you got in."

"Now, now," Mrs. Taylor chided him. "This is the first time Denise has ever broken her curfew. Did you have a good time? I couldn't get much out of you last night. You were on cloud nine."

"Oh, it was great," Denise said. "I met lots of nice kids. I wish Pete had been there. Hey, did he call this morning?"

"Not yet," her mother said, placing a plate of eggs and bacon in front of her.

"I'd better call him now," Denise said. "I want to tell him about the party." She started to rise from her chair, but her mother put a restraining hand on her shoulder.

"After breakfast," she said firmly.

Denise wolfed down her eggs, then went to the phone. She let it ring ten times before she hung up and returned to the table.

"I guess he went with his father to visit his aunt," she said. "Any bacon left?"

She tried him several more times during the

day, but there was no answer. She did her homework, straightened up her room, and waited for Britt to come and watch videos at three o'clock. At exactly two-fifty-five the doorbell rang.

"Am I on time?" Britt gasped, slightly out of breath.

"Precisely," Denise replied, smiling, and beckoned Britt to follow her into the den. Luckily, her parents had gone out for the afternoon, and they had the house to themselves. Denise adjusted the television, and the girls settled back to watch.

"I had a great time last night," Denise told her. "Thanks again for inviting me."

Britt beamed. "No big deal. I knew you'd like the kids."

"I did," Denise replied, and then Ingrid's face flashed through her mind. "Well, most of them."

Britt's face darkened. "You're thinking about Mick, aren't you?" It was more a statement than a question.

Denise shook her head. "No, I wasn't."

But Britt didn't seem to hear. She just sighed. "Lots of kids don't like Mick. He's different, you know?"

At least Denise felt she could respond to this honestly. "Oh, yeah, absolutely."

Britt shook her head and gave a short

laugh. "I'm not stupid. Mick can be pretty rude, and he's not the friendliest person in the world. And sometimes"—she paused as if she didn't want to say the words that then rushed from her lips—"sometimes he's not very nice to me."

Denise couldn't think of a way to ask the next question tactfully, so she just went ahead and said what she was thinking. "Then why do you go out with him?"

Britt didn't respond immediately. She watched the video flashing on the television screen. Her expression was troubled. When the video was over, she turned to Denise.

"There's something about Mick," she said slowly, "that's exciting. Sometimes, when I'm with him, I forget who I am, where I am, what I'm doing. It's like a dream. Do you know what I mean?"

Denise recalled the way she had felt on the terrace with Billy, caught up in the moment, out of touch with reality, doing something she knew she shouldn't do.

"Yes," she said quietly. "I think I do."

They both fell silent as a popular video came on. It was a love song, with a sweet refrain that kept repeating the words, "I'll love you forever, and I'll never let you go." On the screen a guy and a girl held each other tightly, looking incredibly happy.

Denise looked at Britt. Her expression was wistful. "I wish Mick and I could be like that," she said softly.

"What do you mean?" Denise asked.

Britt's eyes were glued to the screen as she spoke. "Happy."

They dropped the subject. Instead, they turned to the videos and the way in which they would present them.

"We could take three examples," Denise suggested. "You know, like a performance video, a story video, and one that's all symbols and weird stuff."

"And talk about how each one interprets the song," Britt added.

"Right!" Denise exclaimed. "Hey, maybe we should tape good and bad examples of each type."

"Great," Britt said enthusiastically.

They tossed different titles back and forth, arguing the pros and cons of various videos. Both girls got excited as they began to realize the possibilities of the project. Denise took notes, and Britt promised to tape the videos on her parents' VCR.

"This is going to be terrific," Britt said as Denise walked her to the door.

Denise agreed. "I think so, too." She stood at the door with Britt. "Listen," she said hesitantly, "I hope everything works out for you and Mick."

Britt looked at her, and Denise thought she saw a hint of sadness in her eyes.

"I just wish I knew how I felt," she said. "Sometimes I feel so confused."

As she closed the door, Denise felt sorry for Britt. What could it be like to go out with a boy who made you feel so insecure? Thank heavens, she had a guy like Pete.

Thinking of Pete, she tried his number again. Still no answer. She wasn't worried because she knew that sometimes Pete and his father spent the whole day at his aunt's. She figured he'd call her when he got home.

Later that evening, after supper, as she laid out her clothes for school and checked to make sure she'd done all her homework, she was aware that something wasn't quite right. It wasn't until she was getting ready for bed that she realized she hadn't talked to Pete all day. She didn't think this had ever happened before—that a whole day had gone by without speaking to him. She glanced at her clock and saw that it was almost eleven. Too late to call. Well, she'd see him at school in the morning. She could hardly wait; she had so much to tell him.

The next morning she dressed and ate breakfast quickly. She wanted to get to school early so she could catch Pete before home-room.

But everything at Lakeside High was different for her that morning. All of a sudden she was no longer an anonymous shadow in the halls.

"Denise, hi!" It was Lucy, the girl she had met at the party, calling to her as she entered the school.

"Hey, Lucy," Denise greeted her.

The chubby girl leaned close to her and whispered, "Did you hear about Jim and Jackie?"

Denise tried to remember who Jim and Jackie were. She vaguely remembered meeting a couple with those names at Britt's party. "What about Jim and Jackie?"

Lucy rolled her eyes. "Well, supposedly they had this humongous fight after the party and almost broke up for good."

"Really?" Denise tried to look interested. But she still wasn't sure if Jackie was the short girl with dark hair in the blue skirt or the girl with freckles in the lacy blouse. "That's too bad," she said politely.

"Oh, it's OK," Lucy said. "They made up and got back together. Hey, there's Susan."

Susan joined them in the hall, and the three girls rehashed Britt's party.

"You really made a hit with Billy," Lucy said. "He couldn't keep his eyes off you all night."

Denise laughed and shook her head. "Billy's a great guy. But he was just flirting."

"Well, you certainly made Ingrid burn," Susan noted. "She looked like she wanted to kill you."

Denise frowned. "Gee, I don't want her to get the wrong impression. I mean, I had fun with Billy, but it was no big deal. You know, I'm going out with Pete Carruthers."

"Don't worry about Ingrid," Susan assured her. "Personally, I think it's about time she realizes she can't just snap her fingers and expect a boy to come running back to her. She wasn't very nice to Billy when they were going out."

Lucy nodded in agreement. "Yeah, and then she just dumped him—for no reason at all!"

Denise shook her head sympathetically. "That's awful. I told Billy about Pete, so he wouldn't think I was leading him on."

"I want to meet this Pete you're so crazy about," Susan said.

Denise remembered her plan to find him before class. She glanced at the clock in the hall. It was too late. The bell was about to ring.

"I'll introduce you at lunch," she promised.

"Great," Susan said. "Bring him over to our table and sit with us."

The bell rang, and the girls separated to go to their homerooms. The morning passed quickly for Denise, and she couldn't believe how differently she felt from the girl who had drifted from class to class unnoticed, only the week before.

In almost every class there was someone she had met at the party. She found herself talking to kids in the halls, walking to classes with girls she hadn't even known on Friday. It felt wonderful! She made a mental note to write a long letter to Courtney that night. Her sister would be so pleased to know that she was finally making friends.

When the time came for lunch, she hurried to the cafeteria. She couldn't wait for Pete to meet some of her new friends. She dashed through the food line, grabbed her tray, and looked for him.

He didn't see her at first. He was sitting there alone, his untouched lunch in front of him, and he was just sort of staring into space, at nothing in particular.

Denise felt love and sympathy flow through her simultaneously. He must have had an uncomfortable weekend with his father, she thought. Quickly she walked over to him and set her tray down across from him.

"Hi," she said brightly.

Pete just looked at her. His expression was

odd—unsmiling, stiff, almost cold. She sat down, and still he didn't say a word.

"I wish you had been there Saturday night," she said lightly. "It was a fantastic party. I had a good time."

"So I heard," Pete said flatly.

What did he mean by that? Was he upset that she went to the party? She decided to ignore it. Maybe he was just in a bad mood.

"Some of the kids I met want us to eat with them," she said, rising from her chair. "Come on, I want you to meet them."

But he didn't get up, and something in his eyes made her sit back down.

"Pete," she asked softly, "what's the matter?"

He looked at her intensely, silently. She felt totally confused. "Are you angry because I had a good time at the party?"

Finally he spoke. "I heard you had a very good time at the party. With Billy Parrish."

She stared at him. "I danced with him, if that's what you're talking about," she said hesitantly. "He's a nice guy, but it was no big deal."

"But you did more than dance with him, didn't you?"

"Huh?"

"I understand you were kissing him. And I wouldn't exactly call that 'no big deal.'"

Denise's mouth fell open, but nothing came out.

"Don't look so surprised," he said dryly. "I do talk to a few people around here."

Denise found her voice. "I—I don't know what you're talking about."

Pete groaned. "Oh, come on, Denise, give me a break." His eyes narrowed. "You know a tall, red-haired girl? Ingrid something?"

Denise nodded.

"Well, she's in my chem class. And she was full of information this morning."

Denise gasped. "She's—she's a creep! She was going out with this guy, Billy, and they broke up, but now she wants him back, so when she saw him dancing with me—"

"Look," Pete interrupted. "Did you or did you not kiss him?"

"Well, sort of, but—"

"OK," Pete said. "At least you're honest."

"Wait a minute," Denise pleaded. "It's not the way it sounds—"

"Oh, no? Look, the way I figure it, when you're going out with one guy, you don't run around kissing other guys."

"I wasn't running around kissing other guys! If you'll just give me a chance to explain—"

"There's nothing to explain. I guess getting into the jet set means more to you than I do."

"No! That's not true!" she exclaimed, but Pete was standing up.

"Forget it," he said gruffly. He picked up his tray and left.

Denise just sat there, stunned. Her thoughts were in chaos. What happened? Why wouldn't he listen to her? How could he just walk out of her life like that?

She looked down at the untouched lunch in front of her and pushed it away. Suddenly she wasn't hungry anymore.

Chapter Seven

Denise sat at her desk. The sun was just beginning to go down, and there was a pretty view of the sunset just outside her bedroom window. But she was oblivious to it. She was hunched over a piece of stationery, trying to describe to her sister the way she was feeling.

The past few days have been awful. I still can't believe Pete broke up with me like that. And he won't even talk to me! I tried to call him yesterday, and he said there was nothing to discuss. He practically hung up on me. How can I make him believe that kissing Billy didn't mean anything? I don't even know why I did it. I guess I just got carried away in all the excitement at the party. Oh, Courtney, I'm so miserable. I miss Pete so much.

And I don't know what to do to get him back. Maybe when you come home, you can give me some advice.

She paused and put her pen down. Just writing about Pete was making her feel even worse. She got up and paced the room restlessly. Surely there was something she could do to make him understand. An idea began to grow. . . . OK, he wouldn't listen to her. But maybe if she wrote him a letter, she could try to explain what really happened at Britt's party. She just hoped he'd read it and not tear it up.

She went back to her desk, pulled out another piece of stationery and wrote, "Dear Pete." Then she stopped and began chewing on the end of the pen. How should she start?

Deep in thought, she was dimly aware of the phone ringing. She practically jumped when she heard her father calling her name.

"Denise? It's for you!"

She leaped up and dashed downstairs. Maybe it was Pete! Maybe he'd finally come to his senses!

She picked up the kitchen phone. "Hello?"

"Denise, hi!"

Britt's bubbly voice sent a rush of disappointment through Denise. She tried not to let her voice show it. "Oh, hi, Britt."

"Listen, are you coming over tonight?"

Denise went blank. "Huh?"

Britt gave an exasperated groan. "Remember? We're supposed to meet tonight to choose the videos we're going to tape for the project."

"Oh, yeah, I forgot."

Britt's voice sounded concerned. "Denise, are you OK? You've been so out of it the past few days."

Denise closed her eyes. She hadn't told anyone about Pete, hoping that he'd get over his anger. But maybe it was time she started facing the facts.

"Pete and I broke up," she said flatly. There was a moment of silence on the other end.

"Gee, Denise, I'm sorry."

The obviously sincere sympathy in Britt's voice didn't help her feel better. In fact, she could actually feel tears beginning to well up in her eyes. Hastily she brushed them aside.

"You're right," she said quickly. "We do need to decide on the videos. I'll be over around seven-thirty, OK?"

She hung up the phone, then stood there, silently, as a tear slowly worked its way down her cheek.

"So that's why Pete hasn't been around."

Denise turned and saw her mother standing there.

"Honey, I didn't mean to eavesdrop, but I

couldn't help overhearing what you said to Britt. Why didn't you tell me?"

"I—I hoped he'd come back," Denise managed to say before bursting into tears. Her mother put her arms around her and hugged her tightly. Denise cried on her mother's shoulder till she felt there were no more tears left.

"I'm OK, Mom, really," she said weakly. "I guess I just needed a good cry."

"Do you want to tell me what happened?" her mother asked gently. Denise hesitated and finally, with a minimum of detail, described the events at Britt's party.

"I guess Ingrid wanted to get even with me for spending so much time with Billy. So she told Pete how she saw Billy and me kissing." She gave a short, brittle laugh. "And I'm sure she exaggerated it a lot, to make it sound like a passionate embrace."

Mrs. Taylor shook her head sympathetically. "Maybe Pete just needs time to cool down. Then he'll listen to you."

"Maybe," Denise murmured doubtfully.

"Besides," her mother added, "this might not be such a terrible thing after all. Now that you're getting to know all these other kids, you might want to start dating other boys."

"Mom!" Denise exclaimed. "I'm in love with Pete! I don't want to go out with anyone else."

"What about this boy at the party? What's he like?"

"Billy?" Denise shrugged. "Oh, he's nice, I guess, and pretty cute, but—I don't know. I just don't feel anything when I'm with him."

"Well, you don't have to be in love with him to go out with him."

Her mother's words stayed with her, and she thought about them as she walked up the driveway to Britt's house. Would she want to go out with Billy Parrish? The idea neither excited nor repelled her. The notion of going out with anyone but Pete left her feeling pretty cold.

Britt opened the door, and her smile was warm. Denise managed a weak one in return.

"Come on in," Britt said. "Gee, you look so down. I know you must be feeling awful about Pete."

Denise admitted she was pretty depressed. "I still can't believe he won't give me a chance to explain. He doesn't even know Ingrid. Why would he be so quick to believe her?"

The girls settled in Britt's ornate den, which looked more like an old-fashioned parlor in a manor house.

"Ingrid's pretty good at convincing people of anything," Britt said. "She's got a real mean streak, but if you don't know her well, she can make you believe she's terribly honest and sincere."

Denise looked at her curiously. "If she's so mean, how come you're friends with her?"

Britt shrugged. "We're not friends, really. But we've always hung out with the same group, and when she was dating Billy, Mick and I used to double with them a lot."

"Oh." Denise glanced at her watch. "I have to be home by nine, so we'd better talk about this project."

"OK," Britt agreed and picked up a tablet and pen from the coffee table. "I was thinking—maybe we could show the Bruce Springsteen one as an example of a performance video."

"Sounds good to me," Denise said listlessly. She was finding it hard to drum up her former enthusiasm for the project. Britt suggested a few other titles, and Denise just kept on agreeing. Actually Britt's ideas were pretty good, and the real work would come later, when they had to decide what they would say about each one.

"All right, I think we've got a good list," Britt said briskly. "I'll watch MTV for a couple of hours tomorrow and tape the right ones."

Denise nodded. Britt eyed her keenly.

"You're not even listening to me."

Denise raised her eyebrows. "I know. I'm

sorry, Britt. But the more I think about Pete—"

"The sadder you get?"

"Mmm—and something else, too." Denise sat up straighter. "You know what? I think Pete's acting like a real jerk."

"That's what it sounds like to me," Britt admitted.

Denise rose from the couch and paced the room. Then she whirled around and faced Britt.

"You know, Pete and I have been going out for three months. And he doesn't even trust me enough to listen to my explanation! He just dumps me." She snapped her fingers. "Like that!"

"That's pretty rotten," Britt agreed. "If Mick ever did that to me—"

"What would you do?" Denise asked curiously.

"I'd cry," Britt replied honestly. "But then I'd get pretty mad."

Denise nodded, and she felt that spark of anger in her grow. Who did he think he was, anyway?

"I'll tell you, Britt, it would serve him right if I did go out with Billy! If he wants to be a loner, let him see what it's like to be really lonely. I'm certainly not going to beg him to come back to me."

"That's the spirit!" Britt exclaimed. "And after what Ingrid did to you, it would serve *her* right if you and Billy started dating."

Getting revenge on Ingrid hadn't occurred to Denise, but she had to admit the notion was strangely appealing. Denise had never been one to hold a grudge, but maybe, just maybe, this was a time to get even.

The phone was ringing, and Britt got up to answer it.

"Hello?" There was a pause, and then Britt's voice became softer. "Hi, honey."

It must be Mick, Denise thought. She pretended to be glancing through a magazine, but she couldn't help overhearing Britt's end of the conversation.

"Denise is here—remember, you met her at the party—No, they're out—Really? Great! See you then. Bye." She hung up and turned back to Denise happily. "Mick's coming over!"

Denise looked puzzled. "I thought you weren't allowed to see him on weekday nights."

Britt looked down and pushed her hair behind her ears. "My parents are out. And what they don't know won't hurt them."

Denise raised her eyebrows. Britt paused and then gave her a slightly embarrassed smile.

"Look, I don't like going behind their backs. But what am I going to do? I love Mick!"

Denise nodded. "Yeah, I guess I know what you mean. I feel—I mean, I *used* to feel the same way about Pete." She got up and gathered her pocketbook and jacket. "Well, if Mick's coming, I guess I'd better be going."

"No!" Britt said quickly. "I didn't tell you the rest. He's not coming alone."

"Huh?"

"Billy's coming with him!" she announced triumphantly.

Denise's mouth fell open, and she sank back down on the sofa. "Oh, Britt, no!"

Britt's forehead wrinkled. "What's the problem? You said yourself, it would serve Pete right if you started dating Billy."

"Yes, but wouldn't that be sort of like using Billy?"

Britt groaned. "You're just going to date him, not marry him. Look, you like Billy, right?"

"Well, sure," Denise said hesitantly. "I mean, who wouldn't? He's nice and cute—"

"And he obviously likes you," Britt continued. "You don't have to be madly in love with someone just to go out with him."

That's what her mother had said. And again she felt that same strange, disturbing sensation she had felt a few minutes earlier. She giggled nervously. "And if Pete gets upset, that's just too bad."

"And Ingrid's going to be furious!" Britt pronounced, with a wicked little grin. "Come on, let's fix our hair."

They barely had time to freshen their lipstick before the doorbell rang. Billy looked terrific. The football jersey he was wearing showed off his broad shoulders, and Denise liked the way his eyes lit up when he saw her.

Mick uttered a brief greeting, kissed Britt casually, and then flung himself down on an armchair.

"Hey, baby, how about getting me something to drink?" It was more a command than a request.

"Sure, Mick," Britt said. "How about you, Billy?"

"No, thanks," Billy said and sat down on one end of the sofa. Britt left the room, and Denise sat down tentatively at the opposite end of the sofa. There was an uncomfortable silence.

"What have you and Britt been up to?" Billy asked her.

"We're working on a project together. It's about music videos."

"Oh, yeah? What class is it for?"

"Sociology. Ms. Cooper's class."

Mick made an ugly sound. "That old bag. She practically flunked me."

Billy laughed. "Can you blame her? You hardly ever showed up in class."

Mick shrugged. "School's a drag."

Billy threw up his arms. "True—but you got to put up with it if you want to play ball."

Britt returned with a soda for Mick and perched on the arm of his chair. The conversation picked up a little then as they began talking about somebody at school who had won a big scholarship to an Ivy League college.

"That guy's a nerd," Mick said.

"Maybe, but he must be pretty smart if he won that scholarship," Britt said. "I hope I can get into a good college."

Mick groaned. "How can you even think about college? I just want to get out of *this* jail."

"What about you?" Denise asked Billy. "Where do you want to go to college?"

"I don't know," Billy admitted. "I mean, my grades aren't that great, but I figure I can get a football scholarship somewhere."

Denise glanced at her watch. "Oh, wow, it's almost nine. I'd better get going. I'm going to be late as it is."

"Hey, I can drive you home," Billy offered.

Denise hesitated. She was supposed to call her father to come get her, but she knew he wouldn't mind as long as she got a ride.

"OK," she said. Mick and Britt were gazing

deeply into each other's eyes and obviously were happy to be left alone. They barely heard Denise's goodbye.

Once in the car, Billy turned to Denise. "Do you have to go straight home?" he asked. "I thought maybe we could get a hamburger or something."

"Thanks," Denise said politely. "But I really do have to get home."

"Oh, right," Billy said as he backed the car out of the driveway. "I forgot. You've got a serious boyfriend, right?"

Denise decided to be bold. "Not anymore," she said lightly. "We broke up."

Billy took his eyes off the road just long enough to give her a pleased look.

"Oh, yeah? Gee, that's too bad, I guess. But, hey, maybe it's good news for me. You want to go out Saturday night?"

Denise paused. She knew she'd be crazy not to accept. After all, it wasn't as if she had a boyfriend anymore. And she'd probably have a nice time with Billy—at least, a better time than she'd have moping around the house, thinking about Pete.

Yet something held her back, something that was keeping her from saying yes automatically. If she went out with Billy, it would be admitting to herself that Pete was actually out of her life. It would be like closing a door.

But maybe she'd better go ahead and close that door. Pete was gone, and she knew she had to face it.

"OK," she said softly. "I'll go out with you, Billy."

When they got to her house, he walked her to the door. "Well, I'll see you Saturday. Around seven-thirty?"

"OK," Denise said again. He bent forward as if to kiss her, and she turned slightly so the kiss would land on her cheek.

"Good night," she said quickly and went into the house. Once inside, she took a deep breath. Well, she had done it; she had made a date with someone other than Pete. OK, maybe Billy wasn't as smart as Pete, or as interesting, but he was nice and good-looking, and he'd make a perfectly respectable date.

But suddenly she remembered the first time Pete had asked her out, how excited she'd been, how she had felt a special thrill run through her at the very thought of being with him. She wasn't feeling anything like that now. And she wondered if she'd ever feel that special thrill again.

Chapter Eight

As Denise picked up her lunch tray the next day, her eyes involuntarily shifted to the table where she and Pete used to sit. He wasn't there, in his usual place, and it dawned on her that she hadn't seen him in the lunchroom at all since they had broken up. She wondered where he'd been eating.

Stop that, she told herself firmly. *It's none of your business. He's not your boyfriend anymore.* And she tried to ignore the ache in her heart as she walked briskly to the table where Britt, Lucy, and Susan were sitting.

"Susan's having a party a week from Saturday," Lucy announced happily as Denise sat down.

"Maybe," Susan cautioned her. "I haven't even asked my parents yet. I think they'll say yes, though. I haven't had a party in ages."

"Are you going to invite Ingrid?" Britt asked. She was looking down at her plate as if she were seriously studying her food.

"Sure, I guess so," Susan said, looking puzzled. "Why do you ask?"

Britt looked up with a sort of resigned half smile on her face.

"She's really been getting on my nerves lately," she admitted. "She keeps asking me these questions about Mick. Like, what sort of music he likes, and where he hangs out after school. It's probably just my imagination, but I can't help but think she's got her beady eyes on him."

Lucy brushed that aside. "I wouldn't worry. Ingrid's interested in anything that looks remotely male."

"Look," Susan said, "none of us are crazy about Ingrid, right? But she's been part of our group for three years, and I don't see how I can have a party without inviting her. She'd be sure to find out, and"—she gave a mock shudder and a short laugh—"I really don't want to get on her bad side."

Denise turned to Britt. "Anyway, if Mick really loves you, he won't pay any attention to Ingrid if she starts flirting with him."

"I know," Britt said, but there was uncertainty in her voice.

"Speak of the devil," Lucy muttered.

Denise looked up and saw Ingrid sauntering toward their table. She had to admit that this girl was awfully good-looking with her flaming red hair and skintight jeans. But there was something about her that kept her from being really pretty, something hard and cold.

"Hi, everyone," she drawled as she settled down directly across from Denise. A ragged chorus of unenthusiastic responses greeted her. Ingrid focused on Britt.

"I just saw Mick leaving school with a couple of other guys."

Britt feigned nonchalance. "Mick can't handle cafeteria food."

"He looked terrific," Ingrid continued. "I love seeing guys in leather jackets. So sexy."

Britt's eyes narrowed, and her forehead wrinkled. She looked as if she were about to say something when Susan hastily entered into the conversation.

"I think I'm going to have a party in a week," she said to Ingrid. "Denise, why don't you bring Pete? I still haven't met him."

Denise shook her head ruefully. "I'm afraid you'll have to find some other way to meet him. We broke up." Without even looking, she knew that Ingrid was smirking.

Britt spoke up brightly. "Billy will probably ask you to the party. By the way, we're going to be doubling this Saturday night. You and

Billy, and Mick and me." She shot a triumphant look at Ingrid, and Denise felt a wicked sense of satisfaction in seeing Ingrid's face drop.

Later that afternoon as she was gathering stuff from her locker to go home, she saw Pete coming down the crowded hallway. For a second her heart stopped. Was he coming to talk to her? But he was engrossed in conversation with some guy and didn't even see her.

She stared after him, resisting an urge to call out. She wished her angry feelings toward him would come back, but it was impossible. All she felt was that dull, throbbing hurt. And it stayed with her, all the way home.

Her spirits lifted a little when she got home and her mother announced some welcome news.

"We got a postcard from Courtney," she said. "She'll be home Saturday, instead of Sunday. She's getting a ride with a classmate."

"That's great," Denise said happily. Then she remembered something, and her face fell. "Oh, no, I almost forgot. I've got a date Saturday night. Maybe I can break it."

"Who's your date with?" Mrs. Taylor asked, looking interested.

"Billy Parrish, the guy I met at Britt's party."

Her mother raised her eyebrows. "Is that the

one you danced with all night and who brought you home the other evening?"

And kissed, Denise added silently. "Yeah," she said. "That's the one."

"You haven't told us much about him," her mother said. "What's he like?"

"Nice," Denise replied idly. "Tall, blond, good-looking. He's on the football team."

Her mother looked quizzical. "You don't sound very excited about him."

Denise grimaced. "I don't know. He's OK, I guess. We don't have much in common, though. All he ever talks about is football."

Her mother laughed. "I went out with a fellow like that in college, before I met your father. I learned more about football than I cared to know."

Denise glanced at Courtney's postcard. "I guess I'm more excited about seeing Courtney," she said. "Maybe I'll call Billy—"

"I don't think you have to," Mrs. Taylor said. "Courtney will probably be tired after that long drive from college, and she may want to go to bed early. Besides, she'll be here a whole week."

"I guess you're right," Denise said. "It's sort of short notice to break a date, anyway."

Her mother put her arm around her. "I think it's good that you're starting to see other boys," she said. "You can't sit around and brood over Pete."

Denise nodded. Her mother was probably right. And it wasn't as if Billy was so bad—he just wasn't Pete.

But she had so much to tell Courtney. She'd never finished that letter she was writing to her. It was hard, trying to write about Pete. Maybe talking about him would be easier. And Courtney had so much more experience with boys than she did. Maybe she'd have some advice.

"What time is Courtney supposed to get here?" Denise asked on Saturday afternoon, glancing out the front window for what must have been the millionth time.

Mr. Taylor checked his watch. "Well, she was supposed to leave sometime before noon. It's a five-hour drive, and they'll probably stop for lunch. I would say six at the earliest."

Denise groaned. Billy was picking her up at seven-thirty. That would give her an hour, at the most, with Courtney.

But six o'clock came and went, and no Courtney, so Denise figured she'd better get ready for her date. She took a shower, washed and dried her hair, and stood in front of her closet, looking at her clothes. It didn't take her long to pick out some jeans and a lightweight red jersey. She put on some mascara and lip gloss and gave herself a quick once-over in the full-length mirror. Then she dashed down to the den, where her parents were watching the news on television.

"Ready so soon?" her father asked. "It seems to me it used to take you hours to get ready for a date."

Denise was spared having to reply when they all heard a car honking outside. She ran to the window. "She's here!"

The slender, sophisticated-looking girl who emerged from the car with a suitcase and a backpack waved frantically as Denise ran out to greet her.

"You've cut your hair!" she exclaimed.

Courtney patted her short, chic hairdo. "How do you like it?" she asked as she gave her sister a hug.

Denise stepped back and surveyed her. People always said Denise and Courtney resembled each other, but Denise couldn't believe that. No matter what Courtney was wearing, she looked elegant. That day, for example, all she had on were simple jeans and a striped T-shirt—nothing special, but as usual, they looked special on Courtney.

Denise grabbed Courtney's suitcase, and they headed for the door, where their parents were waiting. "You look wonderful," Denise said admiringly.

"You, too" was all Courtney had time to say before being engulfed by parental hugs and kisses.

"You must be starving," Mrs. Taylor said. "Why don't you stash your things upstairs, and I'll whip up some dinner."

Mr. Taylor reached for Courtney's suitcase, but Denise grabbed it first. "That's OK, Dad, I've got it.

"I've got so much to tell you," she said as they went into Courtney's room. She looked at her watch and made a face. It was almost seven-thirty.

"I wish I didn't have a date tonight."

"Hey, am I finally going to get to meet the wonder boy Pete?" Courtney asked gaily. "You wrote me so much about him, I feel like I know him already."

"No," Denise said wistfully. "My date isn't with Pete. We broke up."

Courtney paused in the midst of unpacking. "Oh, no! What happened?"

Before she could respond, Denise heard the doorbell downstairs. "I'll tell you all about it tomorrow," she said. Her father's voice drifted upstairs. "Denise! Your friend is here."

"I've got to check this guy out," Courtney

said and followed Denise out of the room. "Who is he, anyway?"

"Just a guy," Denise replied. She walked downstairs to the den.

Billy was waiting for her, standing there awkwardly with his hands in the pockets of his football jacket. Denise tried to work up a little enthusiasm in her voice as she greeted him.

"Hi, Billy. This is my sister, Courtney. She's home from school for spring break."

Courtney thrust out her right hand and Billy shook it.

"Where are you at school?" Billy asked.

"State U."

Billy nodded approvingly. "They had a great season last year. How do you think they're going to do this fall?"

Courtney's forehead wrinkled. "Do what?"

"In football!"

"Oh." Courtney pretended to think. "Sure—I guess they'll do OK." As Billy said goodbye to her parents, Courtney looked at Denise, rolled her eyes, and hissed, "I've never been to a football game in my life."

Denise winked at her, mouthed, "Neither have I," and left with Billy.

"Wow, your sister's gorgeous," Billy exclaimed as they walked to the car. And then he added, "She looks like you."

Denise smiled and took his hand. He really was a sweet guy.

Mick and Britt were in the backseat. Britt greeted her cheerfully, Mick uttered his usual grunt that passed for a "hello," and they were off.

It wasn't a bad evening. On the way to the movies, Denise asked Billy about Lakeside's star quarterback, who had injured his shoulder during the last season. That kept him talking for the whole ride, and Denise managed to ignore the smooching sounds in the backseat.

The movie was good. It was a comedy, and Denise was in the mood for a good laugh. At least it took her mind off Pete for a while. About halfway through, she realized Billy was holding her hand. Suddenly she felt a little depressed. When Pete used to take her hand in the movies, she would feel so thrilled. But tonight she hadn't even noticed when Billy's hand touched hers!

After the movie they went to Gino's for pizza. The restaurant was crowded, but they managed to find a booth in the back.

"What do you guys want on your pizza?" Billy asked. "Pepperoni and peppers? I'll go order." He went off in search of a waitress.

Suddenly Mick got up. "I just decided, I want mushrooms too," he said and walked off in search of Billy. Britt stared after him for a minute, then turned to Denise.

"I taped the videos," Britt said. "Now we just have to decide what we're going to say about each one."

"Why don't we take turns talking," Denise suggested. "We'll show one video, and I'll talk about it, then you'll talk about the next one, and so on."

"That sounds good to me," Britt said. "Let's get together Monday after school, and we can get organized."

"OK," Denise agreed. "I can talk about the Bruce Springsteen video, I've seen it a million times. Then you can talk about Duran Duran." She paused. Britt didn't seem to be listening. She was staring at a table in the corner of the restaurant, and Denise followed her eyes.

Ingrid was sitting there with another girl, and Mick was talking to them. Then he sat down, the other girl drifted away, and he whispered something to Ingrid. Their heads were bent close together, and Ingrid seemed to be laughing.

Denise glanced at Britt, to see how she was reacting. Her face was frozen.

"I need to fix my hair," she said suddenly. "Want to come with me?" Britt's hair looked perfect, and her voice was nonchalant, but something in her eyes begged Denise to join her. Denise rose, just as Billy returned to the table. She told Billy she'd be right back and followed Britt, who was already walking rapidly toward the ladies' room.

Britt was staring at herself in the mirror when Denise entered. She pulled out a brush and began pulling it through her hair furiously. "I can't stand that Ingrid," she said angrily.

Denise wasn't sure how to respond. Ingrid was flirting with Mick, sure, but Mick had a mind of his own. He didn't *have* to talk to Ingrid. But that obviously wasn't the way Britt wanted to look at it.

"She's pretty pushy," Denise said mildly.

Britt was gripping her brush so tightly that her knuckles had turned white.

"Well, she'd better stop throwing herself at Mick," she declared. She turned and looked at Denise as if she expected her to offer some advice. Denise felt torn. Should she say what she was thinking? Should she tell Britt that Mick wasn't worth getting all torn up over?

"Britt," she began hesitantly, "maybe it's not all Ingrid's fault. Maybe Mick—" She stopped when she saw Britt's expression. Britt obviously didn't want to hear what she was about to say.

"Forget it," Britt said, tossing her brush back into her purse. "Let's go. I'm starving."

When they returned, Mick was back in their booth with Billy, and the pizza had just arrived. Britt didn't say anything about Ingrid, and neither did Mick. For a while they ate in silence. Then someone in the restaurant put a quarter in the jukebox, and the room began to throb with music.

Britt wrinkled her nose. "I hate heavy metal." Billy began a friendly argument with her, and that kept the conversation going for a few minutes. Then, somehow, Billy managed to change the subject to football. Britt wasn't saying much, Mick kept glancing over toward the table where Ingrid was sitting, and Billy was giving a blow-by-blow replay of some game he had seen on TV.

Denise stifled a yawn and looked at the clock. "It's almost eleven-thirty," she said with exaggerated alarm. "I've got to get home." That wasn't quite true. She didn't really have to be home till twelve-thirty. But nobody seemed to object to cutting the evening short, and Billy took Denise home first.

"Susan says she might have a party next Saturday," Billy said as he walked her to the door. "Want to go?"

Denise hesitated. She wasn't sure if she wanted to commit herself a week in advance.

What if Pete called? She was still hoping Courtney would come up with some surefire advice on getting him back.

"Maybe," she said tentatively. "But, uh, why don't we wait and see if her parents say yes? I mean, she's not even sure if she's actually going to have the party."

"OK," Billy said easily. "See you Monday." Again he moved to kiss her, and again Denise shifted her head away slightly. But Billy was prepared this time; he shifted, too, and managed to plant the kiss squarely on her lips.

It wasn't an awful feeling. It just didn't feel like much of anything at all. As Billy had said at the party: "No big deal."

"Thanks, Billy."

"Hey, no sweat. I *like* kissing you."

Denise resisted the urge to laugh. "No, Billy, I meant thanks for the evening. Good night."

Once inside the house, she leaned against the door and shook her head ruefully. Billy *was* sweet—not too bright, maybe, but sweet.

The house was quiet, and she figured everyone was asleep. But once upstairs she saw a light coming out from under the door of Courtney's room. She rapped lightly.

"Come on in." Courtney was sitting up in bed, reading a book.

"I thought you'd be asleep," Denise said.

"I guess it's the excitement of coming

home," Courtney said. "I couldn't sleep." She patted the edge of the bed. "Come talk to me."

Denise settled on the bed, and Courtney closed her book.

"It's nice being here," she said. "Peaceful. At school it's always so frantic."

"But you sound like you're having a great time," Denise said. "From your letters it seems like you go to one party after another."

Courtney grinned. "Yeah, but in between the parties there are classes and studying and writing papers. I had to learn to budget my time." She leaned forward and looked at Denise earnestly. "Life's a lot different in college, you know? Being independent is great—but it's scary, too."

Denise was puzzled. "But I thought you were so happy."

"I *am* happy," Courtney replied. "But it's not all fun and games. There's nobody telling you what to do, but that means you've got to make decisions yourself all the time, about everything from classes to who you're going to go out with Saturday night."

"What about that guy you wrote me about, Sam? Is he someone special?"

Courtney shrugged. "He's a nice guy, but we're not serious. I've been dating a lot of different guys." She paused thoughtfully. "You know, in high school I always thought it was important to have one steady boyfriend and not date anyone else. Now, it's more interesting just to go out and have fun and not get too serious."

We're so different, Denise thought. Aloud, she said, "I like the idea of having one special boy."

Courtney smiled. "Billy seems like a nice guy."

Denise nodded. "Yeah, he's nice. But he's not Pete."

Courtney smiled sympathetically. "Tell me what happened."

Denise started slowly, but then the whole story rushed out: Britt's party, Billy, Ingrid, Pete's refusal to listen to any explanation.

"First I felt so hurt, then I got angry. So I figured it would serve Pete right if I did start dating Billy. But now, I just feel so sad all the time. Pete still won't talk to me, and I feel like I'm using Billy. I guess the only good thing that's come out of all this is that I've finally made some new girlfriends." She sighed deeply. "But that still doesn't make up for not having Pete."

Her sister was listening quietly. When Denise finished, she was quiet for a second, and then she said, "Poor Pete."

"Poor Pete!" Denise exclaimed, "How about poor me?"

Courtney looked at her intently. "Think about it. Think about what Pete's feeling. Everyone deserts him. First his mother—"

"But his mother died!" Denise interrupted. "She didn't leave him intentionally!"

Courtney shook her head. "No, of course not, but sometimes the people who are left behind after a death feel deserted. Then his father withdraws emotionally, he's hardly ever home, and now his girlfriend leaves him."

"But I didn't leave him," Denise insisted. "If Pete would only listen to me—"

"Pete's probably very proud," Courtney explained. "He doesn't want anyone to feel sorry for him. You told me yourself, in your letters, that he's a loner. I'll bet he avoids forming any close relationships because he doesn't want to risk losing anyone else he cares about."

Denise felt totally confused. "How did you figure all this out? You've never even met him!"

Courtney smiled complacently and held up the book she'd been reading. Denise looked at the cover.

"*Contemporary Relationships*," she read. "How come you're reading this?"

"It's for my psych course," Courtney said. "It's all about how people interpret relationships according to their needs."

Denise wasn't sure she understood what

that meant, but Courtney sounded like she knew what she was talking about.

"So what should I do about Pete?"

"Keep after him," Courtney suggested. "Don't give up. He needs to know you haven't really deserted him for your new friends."

"How?"

"Talk to him—"

"But he won't listen," Denise argued.

"Then keep trying," Courtney insisted. "Eventually, he'll have to let his guard down. Just don't give up."

"But I don't want to chase him," Denise protested. "That's so pushy."

Courtney tried to stifle a yawn. "Now I *am* starting to get sleepy. Listen, Denise, you know, deep down, that Pete loves you. But he needs to be sure of your love, and he's too proud to let you know. So what if you're a little pushy? A boy worth having is worth fighting for."

Try as she might, this time Courtney could not suppress a real yawn, and Denise got the message and hopped off the bed. But she looked at her sister curiously. "I thought you were against serious relationships. You just said you'd rather date lots of guys than go out with one person."

Courtney smiled wistfully. "Maybe I just haven't met anyone worth fighting for. You know, Denise, you're lucky. I wish I had someone I could care about as much as you care for Pete."

Denise looked at her wonderingly. For so long she had envied Courtney. And here Courtney was telling her *she* was the lucky one! Impulsively she gave her sister a quick hug.

"Thanks, Courtney. I think you may be right. Pete *is* worth fighting for."

She was still repeating those words to herself Monday afternoon as she waited by Pete's locker—their locker. She managed to chew off two fingernails before she saw him coming up the hall.

But her heart sank when she realized he wasn't alone. A boy and a girl were with him; they looked vaguely familiar. Denise had a feeling she had met them at Britt's party.

She heard the boy say, "OK, I'll see if I can get the bugs out of that program. I'll talk to you later." The boy and girl walked off, and Pete turned toward his locker.

She watched his expression closely as he approached. At first his face registered surprise, and then he started to smile. But then it was as if he suddenly became aware of his own reaction and somehow checked it. Finally his face went blank.

"Hello, Pete," she said softly and stepped aside so he could get to his locker.

"Hello," he said politely. "How are you?"

"I'm OK," she said, gripping her books tightly. "And you?"

"Fine."

No, you're not, Denise wanted to say. *You miss me.* But what she actually said was, "I haven't seen you in the lunchroom lately."

Pete was studying the interior of his locker as if the contents truly fascinated him.

"I've been bringing my lunch and eating in the computer room," he replied. "I'm working on a project with Jim and Jackie."

"Oh." So she was right. Those were the two kids from Britt's party who had had the fight and then made up.

For a brief moment she forgot her own situation and felt pleased that Pete had actually found some other kids to work with.

He pulled out a book and a jacket, slammed the locker door shut, and just stood there. "Well," he said formally, "I've got to get going."

"Pete," Denise said quickly. "Wait. I wanted to tell you—"

"What?"

"I—I've missed you."

Was it just her imagination, or did his expression seem to soften a bit?

"Hey, Denise!" A male voice was calling from

down the hall. Reluctantly, Denise turned and saw Billy waving to her.

"I just talked to Susan, and she says the party's on," he yelled. "So I'll call you and let you know what time I'll pick you up Saturday."

Of all the lousy timing, Denise thought furiously. She turned back to Pete. As she might have expected, the expression on his face was frozen.

"It looks like you haven't missed me all that much," he growled, shifting his books to his other arm.

A fury rose up inside her. "Well, what did you expect me to do?" she asked angrily. "Sit at home and mope? Twiddle my thumbs and wait for you to come to your senses and realize that I—I—"

"You what?"

"I love you, you idiot!" And with that, she whirled around and ran away from him.

The tears were still stinging her eyes as she ran down the front steps of the school to where Britt was waiting for her.

"Where have you been?" Britt asked impatiently. "I've been waiting for ages." Then she noticed Denise's face. "Hey, what's the matter?"

Denise wiped her eyes and told Britt about her encounter with Pete.

"My sister says I shouldn't give up, that sooner or later Pete's going to realize how much he needs me. She thinks he's just too proud to admit it."

"She sounds like she's got some smarts," Britt said and grimaced. "Maybe I should talk to her about Mick."

"Is something wrong?" Denise asked, and silently added to herself, *Besides the fact that Mick's no good.*

"I don't know, maybe I'm just paranoid," Britt said as they started walking to her house. "But I have this weird feeling there's something going on between him and Ingrid."

"But you don't know for sure."

Britt shook her head. "No."

"What are you going to do?"

Britt shrugged. "Nothing. Wait and see, I guess." She smiled faintly. "What are you going to do about Pete?"

Denise sighed. "Well, Courtney says I shouldn't give up. She says a boy worth having is worth fighting for."

"Do you think Pete is worth fighting for?"

Denise didn't even have to think about that before she answered. "Yes. What about Mick?"

There was a long pause before Britt responded. "I—I guess so."

Then she fell silent. She didn't ask Denise for her opinion, and Denise was glad—

because she didn't think Mick was worth fighting for. And something in Britt's voice made her suspect that Britt was beginning to feel the same way.

Chapter Nine

"I can't believe we have to present this project tomorrow!" Britt moaned. "How could Friday get here so soon?"

"We'll manage," Denise replied optimistically, but mentally she echoed Britt's despair. The two girls sat on the floor of the Lelands' den, surrounded by note cards, posters, and record albums. The television screen was displaying one of Denise's all-time favorite videos, but she could barely bring herself to look at it.

"Is your sister still in town?"

Denise nodded. "Yes and no. She went into the city for a couple of days to see some of her friends. She'll be home tonight, and then she goes back to school on Sunday." Her eyes narrowed, and she fixed a stern look on Britt. "Are you trying to change the subject again?"

"You got it." Britt made a face at the TV. "Never in a zillion years could I have ever imagined that I would get sick of music videos."

"I know what you mean." Denise shot a baleful look at the TV. "But we've got to get this thing done. Look—we're not in such bad shape."

She picked up the copy of *Time* magazine lying on the floor. "First, you'll introduce the project. All you have to say is something about how music videos are a"—she racked her brain for the right expression—"a monumental phenomenon that's sweeping the nation."

"Isn't that a bit much?" Britt said doubtfully. "I mean, videos are a big deal, but—monumental?"

"OK, OK," Denise said. "How about just 'a major phenomenon'?"

"Better," Britt said and wrote it down. "Then what?"

Denise flipped through the magazine. "Then you read from this article about the impact of music video stations on viewing habits."

Britt took the magazine from her and put a paper clip on the page. Denise looked around. "Where's that copy of *Rolling Stone*?" She spotted it under an album cover and pulled it out. "Then I'll read from this article, about how music videos have had a major effect on record sales and have created new rock stars."

Britt was scribbling this down. "Right, and then I say, 'Music videos enable the viewer to see, as well as hear, music. A video can interpret a song and give it new meaning.' "

Denise looked at her notes. " 'There are several different types of videos,' " she read. " 'Some are simply performances of a song, some tell a story, and some are—' " She paused and squinted at the page. "I can't even read my own handwriting."

"Something about making no sense at all," Britt said.

"Maybe I should just say, 'Some are more abstract,' " Denise mused. "That way it doesn't sound so negative."

"Good idea."

Denise wrote that down. "OK, there's our introduction. Then we show the Springsteen video and you talk."

Britt read from her page. " 'This video is designed to look like a live concert, but really it isn't. The singer is moving his lips to the record."

"OK—" Denise checked her notes. "Then we show the Duran Duran one, and I talk about how it starts off looking like a live concert, but then there are special effects, and so on. What comes after that?"

Britt leaned over to look at the video cassette box where they had a list of the videos they had taped. "Culture Club," she said, punctuating that with her tenth groan of the evening. "Now, what am I going to say about Boy George?"

Britt looked through the stack of posters and pictures they'd cut out of magazines and pulled out the Boy George poster. She gazed at it thoughtfully.

"I think the picture speaks for itself," Denise said.

Britt laughed. "You know, that was a good idea you had, to get these pictures and album covers."

"We'll put them up all over the classroom," Denise said. "It'll be a total visual experience."

"Yeah," Britt said. "And maybe everyone will be so occupied watching the videos and looking at the posters that nobody will pay any attention to what we're saying."

Denise rolled her eyes. "I don't know. I think Ms. Cooper is going to pay a lot more attention to us than Boy George. And she's the one who gives out the grades."

Britt flipped through the pictures, pulled out Duran Duran, and gazed at it dreamily.

"So gorgeous," she murmured. "We don't have any guys at Lakeside who look like this."

"Mmmm," Denise agreed. "Just a lot of guys who think they do."

Britt picked up another picture and studied it. "Do you think Mick looks like Rod Stewart?"

Denise looked at the picture. "Well, to be perfectly honest, no. Do you?"

"No." Then she grinned. "But *he* thinks he does."

For some reason this struck Denise as terribly funny, and both girls collapsed in giggles. At that moment Britt's mother entered the room.

"Well, I'm glad to see you girls aren't working *too* hard." There was a teasing smile on her face as she spoke, but Britt stopped laughing instantly, and her expression stiffened.

"We *are* working," she said.

Denise looked at Mrs. Leland, then at Britt. Obviously, something was going on. Maybe they had had an argument earlier that evening, she thought.

"How's the project going?" Mrs. Leland asked. Britt didn't respond, so Denise felt she'd better say something.

"Pretty good," she said. "We've just about got it all organized. I only hope Ms. Cooper likes it."

There was an awkward silence. Britt was staring down at her notes as if she found them totally fascinating. Mrs. Leland looked around at the mess all over the floor.

"You've certainly gathered a lot of material," she said.

Britt looked at her briefly. "Don't worry, we'll clean it up," she said coldly.

Denise was almost shocked by the tone in Britt's voice. She imagined what *her* mother would say if Denise spoke to her like that. Mrs. Leland did look like she was about to say something but then thought better of it.

"Fine" was all she said, then began to walk out of the room. But at the doorway, she turned back toward them. "Britt, I'm going to the cleaners tomorrow. Is there anything of yours that you want me to bring?"

Britt didn't reply. She just shook her head.

"I thought there might be something special you'd want to wear for Susan's party," her mother added.

Britt turned and looked stonily at her mother. "No."

Mrs. Leland looked at her keenly for a moment and left the room.

"Whew," Denise breathed. "What was that all about?"

Britt drew her knees up to her chest and hugged them. "We had a fight."

"So I gathered," Denise said dryly. "What about?"

Britt's face reflected a strange mixture of resentment and shame. "She and my father were out last night," she said. "So Mick came over. But then they came back sooner than I expected and found us here."

"Wow!" Denise exclaimed. "What happened? Did you get grounded?"

"No, thank goodness. But now they say I can't see Mick at all anymore."

Denise tried to drum up some real feelings of sympathy, but secretly she was almost glad. There was something about Mick that really bothered her.

"Does Mick know?" she asked.

Britt nodded. "He said it doesn't matter. He says we can always get together behind their backs." As she was saying this, she lowered her eyes as if the very words embarrassed her.

Denise was silent and debated saying her next words. She'd only known Britt a few weeks. Were they close enough friends for her to say what she wanted to say? She decided to take the risk.

"Britt," she asked slowly, "is Mick worth it? Like, I mean, worth lying to your parents? You told me before that it's not the best relationship in the world."

"I know," Britt said in a voice so soft Denise had to strain to hear her. "It's funny. Last Saturday when I saw Mick flirting with Ingrid at

Gino's, I was furious. Later, after we dropped you off, we had a big fight about it. But the crazy thing was, when I got home, I didn't cry about it. I was still angry. It just blew my mind that the guy I was with would go off and flirt with another girl. But I can't honestly say that he hurt me. Am I making any sense at all?"

"I think I know exactly what you mean," Denise said. "For me, with Pete, it was the opposite. I kept trying to feel angry, but all I kept feeling was sad." She leaned forward and faced Britt directly. She took a deep breath and then spoke her mind. "You know what I think? I think you don't really love Mick."

She waited for an explosion from Britt. Instead, Britt just shrugged. "I don't know. Maybe. Maybe not. But I don't want to stop seeing him."

"Why not?"

Britt's mouth was set in a tight line. "That would be like giving in. To *them*."

Denise didn't know how to respond to that. And Britt didn't seem to want to talk about it any more. She got up suddenly, left the room, then returned a minute later with two cans of soda.

"Let's get back to Boy George," she said.

An hour later they were gathering up the notes and pictures from the floor.

"I think we've got a pretty good presentation here," Britt said, and Denise agreed.

"I'll get out of P.E. early tomorrow," she said, "and pick up the equipment from the audio-visual room."

"I've got study hall before class," Britt said. "So I'll ask Ms. Cooper if I can put up the posters and stuff then."

Denise called home to have someone come and pick her up. Courtney answered and said she had just gotten home and that she'd drive over.

As they waited, Denise and Britt talked about Susan's party. "Do you want Billy and me to pick you up?"

"Gee, that'd be great," Britt replied. "I hadn't even thought about how I was going to get there, now that I can't go with Mick." That strange, resentful look passed across her face. "At least, we can be together at the party. My parents can't stop me from seeing him there."

Denise heard Courtney honking outside. "Well, see you tomorrow," she said, then paused at the door. "Britt, I don't know your father, but your mother—well, she doesn't seem so awful."

Britt just shrugged. "See you in class."

"How's the project going?" Courtney asked as Denise got into the car.

"Good," Denise said. "We're all set for tomorrow."

Courtney glanced at her as she drove. "Then how come you look so miserable?"

Denise looked at her sister in wonderment. How did she always know what she was feeling?

"I was thinking about Britt," she admitted. She told Courtney about the problems that Britt was having with Mick and her parents.

"I *know* she doesn't really love him," she said. "So why does she hang on to him like this?"

A faint smile appeared on Courtney's face. "Denise," she said, "remember when, about four years ago, Mom and I used to fight all the time about my clothes?"

Denise thought back. She would only have been about eleven at the time, but she vaguely remembered some raging battles.

"Yeah," she said. "I think so. What's that got to do with Britt and Mick?"

Courtney stopped at a red light and turned to Denise. "Those ragged blue jeans I always wore didn't really mean so much to me. But they were my way of rebelling. For some kids, it's important to rebel against their parents. And if there's nothing at home to rebel against—they invent something."

"So you think Britt's just using Mick to rebel against her parents?"

Courtney nodded. "Sure. I'll bet if her mother said something like 'Gee, Britt, that Mick is such a nice boy, why don't you marry him?' she'd probably drop him instantly."

"But they would never say that," Denise objected. "And Britt's got so much pride. She won't ever want to admit her mother's right about Mick."

"She'll come to her senses eventually," Courtney said. "One day I looked in the mirror and realized how awful those grubby jeans looked—just like Mom always said they did. And one day Britt will see Mick for what he is."

"Pride's a funny thing," Denise mused. "It's pride that's keeping Pete from coming back to me."

"Pride gets you nowhere," Courtney said wisely, giving Denise a sideways glance. "But some people have to learn the hard way. They need a little push before they come to their senses."

"But I did try to tell Pete what I feel," Denise protested.

"Try again," Courtney advised. "If Pete's got any brains at all, he'll get the message. And the same goes for Britt. She'll see the truth about Mick."

*　　*　　*

The truth about Mick. The truth about Mick. The words reverberated in Denise's head as she pushed the cart with the TV monitor in it down the hall. If only Britt could have seen what Denise had just seen.

She had gotten permission to leave P.E. early to pick up the equipment for their presentation. The halls were silent as she walked to the audio-visual room. When she turned the corner, the corridor seemed empty.

But it wasn't. She saw them before they saw her. Mick and Ingrid were huddled in an alcove, in front of an empty classroom. And they weren't talking.

Denise froze. For a second it was Britt's party all over again. It was like watching a repeat of a television show but with a different cast of characters. Instead of Billy and Denise kissing, it was Mick and Ingrid. And Denise had the part that Ingrid had played at Britt's party.

Ingrid saw Denise first, and her face registered shock. That reaction only lasted a second before it was replaced by her usual caustic expression. She eased herself out of Mick's arms.

"Uh, we've got an audience," she murmured. Mick turned, glanced at Denise, and muttered, "I'll see you later." He took off rapidly down the hall.

Ingrid seemed to have regained her composure completely. She sauntered toward Denise, who had been rooted to the spot.

"I'll bet you just can't wait to go and tell Britt all about this," she said sarcastically. "And I'll bet you're just thrilled to have this chance to get even with me."

Denise mustered up all the dignity she could. "I have no desire to get even with you," she said tersely. "And whatever's going on between you and Mick is none of my business." With that, she marched past Ingrid and on to the audio-visual room.

But she was definitely shaken and not quite so sure of herself as she had acted. Should she tell Britt? Maybe knowing that Mick was actually fooling around with Ingrid would force her to confront the truth about him. Or maybe this was something Britt needed to find out for herself.

When Denise arrived with the equipment, Britt was in the sociology classroom, taping posters up on the walls.

"Hi," she said.

"Hi," Denise replied and busied herself with searching for an electrical outlet.

"There!" Britt finished taping up the last poster and joined Denise in the front of the room to survey her work.

"Looks great," Denise said, hoping her voice sounded normal.

Britt glanced at her. "You look funny. Is something wrong? Did you see Pete today?"

"No," Denise said quickly. "I guess I'm just nervous about the presentation," she lied.

"Oh, don't worry," Britt assured her. "We'll be fine. Let's try the tape."

Denise watched as Britt put the tape into the VCR and adjusted the dials. She was still debating whether or not to tell Britt what she had seen. Maybe, as a friend, she owed it to her. . . .

But it was too late. The bell rang, and all the kids began filing in, followed by Ms. Cooper. Britt and Denise took their seats, and Denise pulled out her notes to go over them one last time.

"Today we begin our presentations on popular culture," Ms. Cooper said. "Our first report will be from Britt Leland and Denise Taylor."

Denise and Britt rose, exchanged a look, and went up to the front of the class.

"Today we are going to explore a major phenomenon that's sweeping the nation," Britt began. "Music videos."

Denise was pleased to see the usually bored expressions on her classmates' faces change to ones of mild interest. And when they realized they were actually going to see videos, they looked positively enthusiastic.

Their presentation went smoothly. When they finished, the class applauded, and even Ms. Cooper looked pleased.

"Very nice, girls," she said. "Next, we will hear from Keith Miller and Neal Reilly." Denise tried to concentrate on the boys' presentation, but their topic was the Super Bowl, and Denise was so sick of football talk she wanted to scream. Eventually she succumbed to daydreaming—about Mick and Britt, Mick and Ingrid, Billy, and of course, Pete.

"What are you wearing to Susan's tomorrow night?" Britt asked as they gathered their books at the end of class.

"Oh, I don't know," Denise said vaguely. "Jeans, I guess."

"I've got to come up with something spectacular," Britt said. "It'll be the first time I've been with Mick in ages! By the way, have you seen him? I haven't seen him all day. I hope he isn't cutting classes again."

Denise gulped. "I've got to run," she said hastily, "Look, Billy and I will pick you up about eight tomorrow night, OK?"

Without waiting for an answer, she grabbed her books and dashed out of the room.

Chapter Ten

Denise's hands were trembling as she rolled a lock of her hair around a hot curler. The curler slipped through her hands and fell to the floor, leaving her hair straight and limp. She grabbed another one.

"Ow!" she exclaimed as the overheated curler burned her fingers. She pulled the plug on the unit, sucked on her finger, and glared at her reflection in the mirror.

Why was she so nervous? It was just another date with good old Billy, just another evening of listening to how the Lakeside Tigers were going to mutilate Riverside High next year.

And it couldn't be the party that was making her nervous. Susan's party would probably be exactly like Britt's, and the same people would be there. She was actually looking forward to it, now that she had made some friends and felt that she belonged.

But then why did she feel so jumpy, so apprehensive? Why did she have butterflies in her stomach? And why, why, why couldn't she get the dumb clip fastened securely to the curler?

"Need some help?" Courtney was standing in the doorway.

"Oh, please." Denise shot a grateful look at her sister and turned over the job of hair rolling to her.

"What's the matter?" Courtney asked as she efficiently wound Denise's hair around one curler after another. "You seemed so jittery during dinner."

"I don't know," Denise admitted, frowning. "I just have this funny feeling about tonight. It's like a premonition or something."

"Something to do with Pete?"

"No," Denise replied thoughtfully. "Maybe I'm just thinking about Britt." She had told Courtney what she had seen in the hall the day before. "Do you think I should have told Britt about Ingrid and Mick?"

Courtney shook her head. "No, I think she needs to find out for herself. If she's really in love with the guy, she'll just refuse to believe what you tell her. And if Mick's really fooling around behind her back, she'll find out soon enough."

Denise agreed reluctantly. "I'm just afraid she's going to find out tonight."

Courtney stuck the last clip in Denise's hair and stood back to admire her work. "Then she's going to need a good friend, and possibly a shoulder to cry on," she said.

"I know," Denise said. Then she smiled faintly. "At least, worrying about Britt gets my mind off Pete." She touched the curlers, which had cooled off, and began unwinding her hair.

"Courtney," she asked, "do you think it's wrong for me to be going out with one guy when I'm in love with someone else?"

"That depends," Courtney replied. "Do you think Billy's falling in love with you?"

Denise grinned. "No. Billy's not the serious type." Then her face became sober. "But if he wasn't taking me out, he might find a girl who could care about him more than I do. I just can't help feeling like I'm using him. Oh, Courtney," she moaned, "why has life suddenly gotten so complicated?"

Courtney laughed lightly and started to pull out the rollers. "That's what happens when you start growing up. And let me tell you, kid sister—it doesn't get any simpler."

*   *   *

The door bell rang at seven-forty-five.

"Hey, you look terrific," Billy said happily, and Denise felt a pang of guilt. He was such a nice, sweet guy.

"Do you mind if we stop for Britt?" she asked as they got in the car. "You know her folks won't let her see Mick anymore, so he can't pick her up."

"Yeah, he told me," Billy said. "It's probably for the best."

"Why?"

Billy shifted uncomfortably in the driver's seat. "Well, just between you and me, I think Mick wants to start going with Ingrid."

"I can't stand Ingrid," Denise said angrily. "She's a sneak, and personally, I can't understand why any guy would be interested in her."

Billy chuckled. "Yeah, I figured the girls aren't too crazy about her. But Mick's got a real thing for her, you know what I mean?"

Denise didn't bother to answer that. *Poor Britt*, she thought, and her heart ached for her.

But when Britt emerged from her house, she didn't look as if she needed anyone's sympathy. Denise had never seen her look better. The brown silk shirt deepened the brown of her eyes, and the flowered peasant skirt was feminine and graceful. Her hair gleamed, and the red scarf crossing her forehead gave her a slightly gypsy look.

By comparison, Denise felt almost dull in her gray pants and gray- and white-checked shirt.

Britt didn't say much in the car, and something in her expression kept Denise from asking her if anything was wrong. She looked preoccupied.

The party was in full swing when they got there. Susan greeted them at the door.

"Hi, guys," she said cheerfully. "Come on in!"

Billy and Denise greeted her, but Britt took her aside. "Is Mick here yet?" Denise heard her ask. Susan shook her head.

Unlike Britt's house, Susan's was comfortable and casual. Kids were all over the place, including the kitchen and living room. In the spacious den, furniture had been pushed back for dancing. Susan led Britt and Denise to her bedroom to drop off their pocketbooks and fix their hair. A short, cute girl with curly light-brown hair was sitting at Susan's dressing table.

"This is my cousin, Patsy," Susan said. "Patsy, this is Britt Leland and Denise Taylor."

"Hi!" the girl said brightly.

"Patsy goes to Riverside High," Susan explained.

"And I wish I could transfer to Lakeside!" Patsy's voice was bubbly. "The guys here are so cute! I tell you, when I saw those hunks downstairs, I swear, I almost passed out!"

Britt and Denise exchanged looks, but both managed to keep straight faces.

"Once you get to know them," Britt said dryly, "they're not all that cute."

Patsy looked puzzled for a second, but that didn't last long. "Well, I'm dying to meet them, anyway," she said. "Let's go get 'em, girls!"

Behind her back, Susan rolled her eyes.

Back in the den several couples were dancing, and Billy looked impatient. "Hey, come on, I want to dance!"

Denise was aware of Susan's cousin standing by her side, with her big, brown eyes fixed on Billy.

"Billy, have you met Susan's cousin, Patsy?"

Billy's eyes widened as he took in the new face.

"Hi!" Patsy said, her perky smile getting even perkier.

"Patsy goes to Riverside," Denise added, watching the two of them making eye contact. Something was definitely happening!

"Hey," Billy said, "we clobbered you guys

last year, but I hear you've got a new quarterback."

"We do!" Patsy exclaimed. "He transferred from Madison. And he's fantastic! We're going to have an incredible season this fall. You should see his lateral pass from the line of scrimmage."

"You into football?" Billy asked, his eyes getting even wider.

Patsy smiled modestly. "I'm the new cocaptain of Riverside's cheerleading squad."

As Patsy and Billy discussed the technique of Riverside's new quarterback, Denise let her eyes drift around the room. She saw Susan greeting Jim and Jackie, and someone else with them.

And then it was as if an electrical charge shot through her body. That someone else was Pete.

She didn't want to stare, but she couldn't tear her eyes away. Pete was talking to Susan. Denise couldn't hear what he was saying, but she recognized the expression on his face: polite, pleasant, but slightly uncomfortable.

Denise took a deep breath, touched her hair to make sure the waves were still intact, and slowly made her way toward Pete. He was standing alone when she reached him.

"Hi," she said softly. He looked wonderful. And it wasn't just his face, clothes, and hair. It was something in his eyes she hadn't seen in a long time.

"Hello, Denise."

For a second Denise felt as if they were alone in the crowded room. And then the spell was broken. Billy appeared by her side.

"Hey, are we going to dance or what?"

Denise thought quickly. "Uh, Billy, would you mind if we didn't dance just now? I think I, uh, twisted my ankle or something," she lied.

"OK," Billy said agreeably, but he looked disappointed. Denise introduced him to Pete, and the boys shook hands. Then Denise had an inspired idea.

"Billy," she said suddenly, "why don't you ask Patsy to dance? She doesn't really know anyone here."

Billy brightened instantly. "OK," he said again and drifted off.

"Seems like a nice guy," Pete remarked casually.

"Oh, he is," Denise replied. There was an awkward pause.

"I guess you're wondering what I'm doing here," Pete said.

Denise shrugged. "I'm just glad you're here."

Pete smiled slightly. "I told you I've been working with Jim and Jackie on a computer

project. They asked me to come with them."
He paused. "I wasn't going to come. You know
I'm not big on parties. But then I changed my
mind."

"Why?"

He didn't seem to hear her.

"Pete—" she began. But a voice from across
the room interrupted.

"Hey, Pete!" It was Jim calling him. "Come
over here, I want you to meet someone."

"Look," Pete said quickly, "I want to talk to
you, but I'd better go see what Jim wants." He
bit his lower lip. "Could you meet me
outside?"

"Sure," Denise said happily. "I'll be on the
porch."

She wondered if she should tell Billy she was
going to disappear for a few minutes. But she
spotted him across the room, happily dancing
with Patsy, and figured he wouldn't mind.

She walked out the front door and was
pleased to find the porch empty. It was very
dark, but she didn't mind. She stood there
silently, enveloped in a sense of happy antici-
pation.

But then a car pulled up in front of the
house. Denise just hoped that whoever was in
the car would go directly into the house and
not hang out on the porch.

Two people got out of the car, and in the

darkness Denise couldn't make out who they were—until they got closer to the house. And she felt a sickening feeling in her stomach. It was Mick and Ingrid. And they were obviously together: he had his arm around her, and she was whispering in his ear. Then they stopped and kissed.

As they approached the porch, Ingrid spotted Denise. "Well, well, well," she said in a sarcastic tone. "Look, Mick, it's the little spy again. Waiting to see something to report to your friend Britt."

"That won't be necessary," said a voice from the darkness. Denise turned and gasped. She hadn't even seen Britt standing there in the shadows at the other end of the porch.

Mick's mouth fell open. "Uh, hi, Britt. Ingrid needed a ride, so—"

"I don't care," Britt said harshly. "And I'm not interested. We're finished, Mick. You were never any good for me. And I'm glad I saw you two together. Because now I know that for sure."

She stopped and turned to Ingrid. "You want him, Ingrid? You can have him. I think the two of you deserve each other."

There wasn't the trace of a quiver in her voice, and she held her head high as she whirled around and marched back into Susan's house.

Ingrid seemed to have momentarily lost her composure. "Let's get out of here," she muttered to Mick, and they both walked rapidly back to the car.

Denise felt as though she had just witnessed the climax of a dramatic movie. When she was able to pull herself together, she realized she'd better find Britt right away. She had a feeling, as Courtney had said, that Britt might be in need of a shoulder.

She practically collided with Pete at the door. "Sorry to keep you waiting—" he began.

"Pete," she said in a rush, "I've got to go find Britt. Something's happened, and I can't explain now, but don't leave, OK? Please?"

Pete looked completely bewildered, but he managed a "sure" as Denise raced past him and into the house.

Chapter Eleven

She found Britt in Susan's room, sitting on the bed and staring at nothing. But her eyes were dry, and her face was calm. When she saw Denise, she managed a faint smile.

"I'm OK," she answered before Denise could even ask the question. Denise sat down beside her on the bed.

"It must have been a shock," she said gently. "Seeing Mick and Ingrid like that."

"Yes and no," Britt replied. "I mean, I had a feeling something was going on. I had planned to have a talk with Mick tonight. In fact, believe it or not, I was actually thinking about telling him that I didn't want to see him anymore."

"Because of Ingrid?"

"Not exactly." She looked at Denise. "I know you must think I've been pretty awful, going out with a guy who acts like a creep and sneaking around behind my parents' backs."

Denise started to protest, but Britt stopped her. "I haven't felt very good about myself lately, either. Mick and I never had a good relationship, even from the beginning. But it took a long time for me to realize that I was dating Mick just to spite my parents."

"But you seemed so in love," Denise said.

Britt grimaced. "It's amazing the way I built Mick up in my mind, making him something he's not. You know, you can convince yourself of anything if you concentrate hard enough. And I managed to convince myself that Mick was this wonderful guy, the boy of my dreams. While all the time, he was exactly the sort of jerk my parents said he was."

Denise remembered what Courtney had said about Britt. "Maybe holding on to him was your way of rebelling against your parents."

Britt nodded. "My parents wanted me to date a nice boy. So I decided to find myself a boy who wasn't so nice, someone I knew they wouldn't approve of." She laughed bitterly. "Mick was perfect. A troublemaker, no ambition, no concern for anyone but himself. I was so sick of hearing them talk about my brother, Mister Perfect. My mom and I had a long talk about it today."

"What did she say?"

"She said she'd never realized that I felt like they were always comparing me to my brother." She smiled softly. "She even said she was sorry about it. For the first time in ages, we really talked to each other. I've still got a lot to work out with them. But at least we've made a start."

"That's great," Denise said warmly. Then she felt that she'd better make a confession. "You know, Britt, I saw Mick and Ingrid together on Friday. And I didn't tell you because I was so afraid you'd be hurt."

Britt didn't look surprised. "It doesn't matter. I've been hearing rumors about them all week. I just didn't want to believe them. I guess I needed to see for myself."

"You're really taking this well," Denise said.

Britt shrugged. "I won't say I don't feel hurt." Her eyes became hazy. "There were times when Mick could make me feel very special." She sighed deeply, then shook her head briskly as if trying to shake away the sadness. "But I'll get over it."

Just then Susan appeared at the door. "What's going on?" she asked, looking bewildered. "First Britt disappears, then you leave the scene. I saw Mick's car out front, but then he never showed up."

"He showed up," Britt said flatly. "And he wasn't alone."

Slowly realization dawned on Susan's face. "Oh, no," she said. "You mean, he was with Ingrid? Oh, Britt, how awful!"

"I'll live," Britt assured her. "Mick's a creep, and I'm glad we're finished. But to tell you the truth, I don't feel that much like partying tonight."

Denise hopped off the bed. "Then let's go find Billy, and we'll take you home."

As the three girls headed back to the den, Susan turned to Denise. "Did you see Pete? He came with Jim and Jackie."

Denise stopped suddenly and clapped a hand over her mouth. Pete! She'd left Pete stranded on the porch! In her concern for Britt, she'd forgotten all about him. Her heart sank. Had she just blown her last chance at getting back together?

"There's Billy," Britt said. "He, uh, looks sort of preoccupied." Denise saw what she meant. Billy was still dancing with Susan's cousin Patsy, and it was a slow dance. The two of them were very, very close. Every now and then, the little cheerleader would look up at Billy with adoring eyes. Billy looked as if he were floating on cloud nine.

"Oh, dear," Susan murmured and glanced at Denise uneasily. But Denise just smiled.

"They look happy," she said. "I don't think we should disturb them." Then she had an idea. "Wait here," she instructed Britt. "I'm going to see if I can get us a ride home."

She made her way through the couples dancing in the den. As she passed Billy and Patsy, clinging together with their eyes closed, she couldn't resist a smile. They looked absolutely right together.

The noise of the party faded as she walked out on the porch, closing the door behind her. There didn't seem to be anyone there. She should have known better than to think Pete would just hang around, waiting for her. He probably had gotten tired of waiting and had gone home.

"Denise." The voice from the shadows sent a thrill through her.

"Oh, Pete," she said gratefully. "Thanks for waiting."

"It's nice out here," he said. "It's a little too crowded inside for me. Not that the people don't seem nice," he added hastily. "I guess I'm just not much of a party animal."

"I know," Denise replied. "But I'm glad you're here." She coughed nervously. "I need to ask you a favor."

"What?"

"Britt and Mick broke up, and she wants to go home. But she needs a ride."

"How did she get here?"

Denise was afraid he'd ask that. "She came with Billy and me." Even though it was too dark to see the expression on Pete's face, she had a feeling he wasn't smiling.

"Why can't you and Billy take her home?"

Denise paused and decided she might as well be honest. "Did you meet Susan's cousin, Patsy?"

"No."

"Well, Billy did, and I think he's just found the love of his life. I'd hate to break it up."

"Where does that leave you?" Pete asked.

"I guess I need a ride home, too."

There was a brief silence, and then he said, "OK."

Denise dashed back into the house. Billy and Patsy were still dancing, and she hated to interrupt them, but—

"Billy?" She tapped him on the shoulder. He turned and looked at her with a slightly surprised, and definitely dazed, expression.

"Huh? Oh, hi."

"I have to go, but don't worry, you can stay. I've got a ride."

Billy grinned amiably. "OK," he said. "Bye."

So much for that relationship, Denise thought as she collected Britt and said a quick goodbye to Susan. Well, there was never anything there to begin with—just two nice people not meant for each other. She had a strong suspicion that Patsy would appreciate Billy a whole lot more than she ever had.

"Pete's taking us," she whispered to Britt, and Britt shot her a look of surprise. "I'll call you tomorrow," she added hurriedly. "Maybe with some good news!"

Pete was waiting for them on the porch.

"Hi," Britt said. "I really appreciate this, Pete."

"No problem," he said easily. "I was getting ready to leave anyway." He led them to his car, and Britt immediately got into the backseat. Denise made a mental note to thank her and got into the front seat with Pete.

"Do you want to get something to eat?" Pete asked as he drove away from Susan's. Before Denise could reply, Britt said, "Not me, thanks. I'd better get straight home. I've got a fierce headache. It's been a rough night."

Denise turned to give her a look of concern, and Britt winked. Denise added an exclamation point to her mental thank you.

"Besides," Britt added, "I want to tell my parents the good news."

"Huh?"

Britt smiled, a little proudly, a little wistfully. "No more Mick."

Chapter Twelve

After they dropped Britt off, Pete let the car idle in the driveway. He was staring straight ahead as he spoke. "Do you want to go back to the party?"

"Not particularly," Denise replied.

"Home?"

"No."

Finally he turned and looked directly at her. "Where, then?"

She wasn't feeling terribly sure of herself. "Some place we can talk?" she suggested tentatively. "Maybe get something to eat—"

"I *am* pretty hungry," Pete admitted. "Pizza?"

"OK."

They drove in silence for a while. "I really appreciate your taking Britt home," Denise said. "I know Britt does, too. She's acting pretty cool about all this, but I have a feeling she's more shook up than she'll admit."

"What actually happened?"

Briefly Denise described Britt's relationship with Mick. "And even though she's glad it's finally over, I think she can't help but feel a little sad—"

"Yeah," Pete said. "It's always sad when someone goes out of your life."

Denise looked at him. Was he talking about her? His mother? His father? All of them? But Pete was looking at the road, and his face told her nothing.

Luckily Gino's wasn't too crowded or noisy, and they found a quiet booth in the back.

"Medium pizza with everything, hold the anchovies," Pete told the waitress. "And two Cokes." The waitress jotted down the order and disappeared.

Now that they were there, alone, facing each other, Denise couldn't think of a thing to say. No, that wasn't exactly true. She knew exactly what she wanted to say. She just didn't know how to say it, where to begin. They sat in silence a long time.

"I really was surprised to see you at the party," she finally said. Hadn't she already said that? "And happy," she added.

Pete smiled slightly. "I'll tell you why I

changed my mind and decided to come. I knew you'd be there."

Denise was surprised to feel tears forming in her eyes. This was what she wanted to hear—so why did she suddenly feel like crying?

"Pete," she said weakly, "I've missed you so much. Why wouldn't you even listen to me? Why haven't you called?"

Pete had a faraway look in his eyes. "Pride, I guess," he said. "When you started hanging out with your new friends, I figured you didn't need me anymore." He gave a strange, hard laugh. "You know, when Ingrid told me about you and Billy kissing at the party, I wasn't even surprised. It was as if I'd expected it. I mean, I just had this feeling you'd meet someone at that party."

Denise was puzzled. "But why? Why would you think I'd be even remotely interested in another boy?"

Pete looked like he was trying very hard not to show any emotion. "I just knew I was going to lose you."

Denise looked at him in astonishment. "Why?"

His face was blank, and his next words were barely audible. "Because I seem to lose everyone I care about."

Denise became very still. Then Courtney

was right. Poor Pete felt that his mother had left him when she died, and so had his father, when he continued to mourn. And so he expected Denise to leave him, too—and the smallest rumor could convince him that she had.

Her voice was gentle. "Pete, is that why you're such a loner? Are you afraid that if you start to care about people, they'll end up leaving you?"

Pete nodded. Was that a tear in his eye? If so, it disappeared in a flash as a mask of indifference suddenly covered his face.

"Don't feel sorry for me," he said quickly. "I like to be alone. I don't need anyone."

"That's not true," Denise replied, suddenly feeling very, very sure of herself. "I don't believe you. People need people. Everyone needs somebody to love. You need somebody."

Pete looked like he was about to argue this, but Denise wouldn't let him. She hadn't finished. "You're afraid to love, you're afraid to even make close friends because you don't want to risk being hurt. But there's no guarantee that you won't get hurt, sometime—that's what life's all about. Unless you really want to be alone all your life and build a wall around yourself."

"Well, maybe that's exactly what I do want," Pete said harshly.

"Great," Denise replied, hearing the anger in her own voice. "Then just go right ahead and do that. Don't let anyone trespass on your life. And you'll never be hurt." Then her voice softened, and the anger turned to sadness. "But you'll never be happy, either."

The stillness that followed her words was broken by the sound of a platter slapped down on the table between them.

"One medium, all the way, minus anchovies."

The waitress left, and Pete stared at the pizza. "She forgot the mushrooms."

Denise refused to let her eyes leave his face. "Forget the mushrooms. Pete, have you heard anything I've said?"

Pete carefully lifted a slice of the pizza and bit into it. Then his eyes met hers. "Everything," he said dully. "I heard every word." He put down the slice. "Denise, I never thought I'd admit this. But everything you say is true, and I know it. I guess I've always known it."

Denise knew these were not easy words for him to say. She didn't say anything. She just nodded and hoped her eyes would encourage him to continue.

Pete took a deep breath as if steeling himself to make a confession. "Tonight, at that party, I looked at all those kids, talking and dancing and laughing. And I realized something. I haven't just been alone. I've been lonely. For a long time. I was only happy when I was with you. When I thought I had lost you—" His voice broke off.

Denise leaned across the table. "You never lost me, Pete. I never stopped loving you."

A slow smile spread across his face. "I've really been an idiot, haven't I?"

Denise thought about this for a minute and figured she might as well be honest. "You sure have."

And then they were both laughing, quietly at first, then hysterically.

"Hey, you know what?" Denise asked, still laughing.

"What?"

"I'm starving!"

"Me, too," Pete said. "I think true confessions make you hungry."

They devoured the pizza, and both agreed it was the best they'd ever had. Or maybe it was just the way they were feeling.

"Denise," Pete said as they finished eating. "Things are going to be different from now on. At least, I'm going to try to break down these walls I've built."

"I'll help you," Denise said. "I'll introduce you to people. There are some really nice kids around."

Pete nodded. "What you said before—about

people needing people—you're right. And everybody needs somebody to love."

"Even you," Denise said lightly.

"Even me," Pete agreed. "I love you, Denise. I need you."

Happiness filled her as she gazed into his earnest, loving eyes. "Well," she said, reaching across the table to take his hand, "you got me."

Caitlin

From Francine Pascal, the creator of the SWEET VALLEY HIGH® books, comes something new and very exciting. It's CAITLIN: A LOVE TRILOGY and you won't want to miss it!

Caitlin — she's gorgeous, charming, rich and a little wild; she's the outrageous, dazzling star of LOVING, LOVE LOST, and TRUE LOVE. You're going to want to read all three —just to see what Caitlin will do next as she reaches out for her heart's desire!

For readers who like lots of excitement with their romance and lots of romance with their excitement — CAITLIN: A LOVE TRILOGY! Get it wherever paperback books are sold!

Bantam Books